MY FRIEND KROW

MY FRIEND KROW
© 1977 Fiona Satow
All rights reserved
Scripture Union
47 Marylebone Lane
London W1M 6AX
ISBN 0-85421-510-7

Second printing, July 1981
American edition published by CHARIOT BOOKS
A division of David C. Cook Publishing Co.
© 1979 David C. Cook Publishing Co.

Cover photo by Armadillo/McQuilkin

Printed in the United States of America
ISBN: 0-89191-141-3
LC: 78-75360

My friend KROW

Fiona Satow

David C. Cook Publishing Co.

ELGIN, ILLINOIS—WESTON, ONTARIO

One

"YOU'LL NEED YOUR PARKAS," mom called from the kitchen. "Remember what your dad always says—how much colder it can be right up on the felltop. . . ."

Kate and Nick Braithwaite were listening in the hall. They made faces at each other and giggled. Dear mom, she did fuss so. Nick yanked up the bottom of his T-shirt until it was around his chin and beat a Tarzan drumroll on his bared chest. They were both tall for twelve, dark-haired, dark-eyed, and darkly tanned, now, at the end of one of the hottest summers they could remember. And, like many twins,

7

they were very, very alike.

Kate giggled again, lifting her hands to smother the fun in her face, but Nick could see her eyes glinting between the spread fingers.

"Look, I'll go first up the cliff. Then you can have a go at being leader later on." He knew she'd probably be too scared to lead, anyway, but she'd never admit it.

Their dad was away in the navy. He sent them fabulous postcards of desert islands and exotic tropical cities. But mom was always in one long sulk until he came home again, so the twins tended to gang up against her. The fact that they lived halfway up a mountain in the middle of England's Lake District meant they had few other friends, and mom rarely went out at all. The twins just ran wild on the fells, the elevated wild moors that surrounded their home. They had secret hideouts in the bracken, the large, coarse ferns that abounded in this area. They knew where the foxes hunted and where the tiny, dusky bilberries grew, high up among the mosses and boulders. And somehow it was all much more exciting to keep these things from her.

"Sandwiches are ready," she announced, and the two of them bounded into the kitchen, ravenous enough already to want to know just what she'd prepared for them.

"Meat-paste in the wax paper, cheese in the

plastic bag—and a couple of apples, too. I know you loath carrying thermoses, but if you *are* going to drink from the streams do be careful. I mean, make some effort to check there isn't a dead sheep ten yards upstream—especially at this time of year when the streams are all so low." A tired smile touched her always worried face.

Both of them grinned back, but more because they realized their trip was nearly underway than because they really had any intention of sniffing out dead sheep's bodies before taking an odd gulp from a stream.

"Ready then?" She watched the twins stuff the lunch packets into Nick's knapsack and tie the bulky parkas unwillingly around their middles.

"Would you believe it—*yes!*" They both rushed for the dark hall and the pool of sunshine splashed on the carpet through the window in the front door.

"Hey, just a minute, you two," came mom's stern voice somewhere behind them. "And *what* about your feet?"

Kate and Nick both looked down at their faithful gym shoes, and wiggled their toes in silence through the canvas. There's something about gym shoes: they only last one summer, but by the end of that summer you're really fond of them and your feet are fond of them, too. They're as light and soft as an extra skin.

"Come on now, the two of you. You can't possibly go right up onto Castle How with no more than canvas shoes on your feet. Now do be sensible. Your socks are upstairs in the chest of drawers, and I remembered to get new laces for your boots just yesterday when I was in Moseley."

Out of the corner of his eyes Nick could see that Kate was sucking in her cheeks, which she always did when she was about to give in. But he for one certainly wasn't going to put up with those great, clod-hopping climbing boots in hot, August sunshine. He had a brainwave. "We'll get lousy blisters, mom," he complained. "After all, we've only worn gym shoes most of the summer, and the skin'll have gone all soft around our heels."

"Don't you think socks would be a good idea, then?"

Oh! She was so sensible and reasonable! Nick stared at her—straight in the eyes, as he always did, now that he was as tall as she was. He could never out-argue her, so he would outstare her instead.

She swallowed, and an extra pain tightened the worry-lines on her forehead. He knew what would come next.

"Nicky, don't keep on making me have to say this, but you *know* how your father insists. I do sometimes wonder," she sighed, "if you realize how it hurts me to argue with you like this when you'd obey him in a flash if he were here. . . ."

At this Kate sort of crumpled and dashed upstairs. She took much longer than she would have needed simply to put on her socks, and when she came down again she moved slowly, her head low. Nick knew she'd had a quick cry.

She fetched her boots from the porch, sat down on the stairs, and slowly began to lace them up. Mom and Nick had avoided looking at each other while Kate was upstairs. Now they both watched her—at least it gave them somewhere to look. When the thongs were finally tied behind her ankles, Kate leaned back, stuck her legs out, and grinned at the boots. Nick grinned, too. You had to: great, hulking boots like weights, on the end of long, skinny, brown legs. Good old Kate! They caught each other's smiles, and this gave them courage.

"Right, mom," Nick announced briskly, as if nothing had happened. "We'll be back by teatime." She'd given up battling with him; her energy finished. Realizing they were safe, Nick managed a big, sympathetic smile, and added, "Sorry you can't come, too!" Such a stupid thing to say. Course she couldn't come. Nor did they want her.

"Liar!" hissed Kate as they pounded down the slate-chip garden path.

11

"Same to you!" he tossed back. "Besides you don't really want to lead in the climbing anyway, do you?"

She was quiet for a moment. Then teased him back. "Hey, you mountain goat! Haven't you left something behind?" She stopped sharply by a large rhododendron bush. They were now well out of sight of the windows of the house.

"Mmmm? For the climb?" He couldn't face going back for anything. Not now.

"Well, you tell *me* what this great leader's going to lead me with, then. . . ."

Nick grinned as he realized. "OK, Kate. Look, you stay here. I'll run up through the orchard and into the washhouse that way. Should be safe."

Two minutes later he was back with the beautiful snakelike coils of mom's new, nylon clothesline. The loops were still held into shape by paper ties with the Co-op mark on them.

Kate's eyes danced with a wild thrill. This was easily the most daring thing they'd ever done together. He could tell her excitement was near bursting point. She was really well liked by the other girls at school, but they were always talking about clothes and pop singers. He knew it was only with Nick, like this, that she felt herself . . . wild and free.

They sprinted off again down the path,

Kate's clod-hoppers throwing up rattling flakes of slates, the half-empty knapsack bouncing against Nick's shoulder blades—first one side, then the other. Old Fred, the gardener, looked up from the rock garden at the clatter and waved.

It was hot, high summer, and the bracken was at its tallest, so for the next hour or so the twins set their bodies into the slope and plodded, ached, and strained their way up the narrow sheep tracks.

It was so hot that they didn't bother talking. They knew they got short-tempered with sweat running into their eyes and their knees like plasticine. And what was there to say, anyway? Nick knew Kate's knees would be about as weary as his were.

He'd trained himself never to look up when he was climbing a fellside. If he did he knew he'd think he was nearly at the top, yet as he climbed a little higher a new "top" would always appear until it seemed that he'd never reach the real top.

However, soon the bracken thinned and finally died out altogether. They were high up, now. Their feet wandered freely over coarse, springing tufts of grass, stretching around and above them in a great sun-drenched, pale yellow expanse. There was no path now, but they knew their direction well enough—up, still!

At last they toiled over the final, swelling breast of the fell. It dipped, beyond, into a large hollow in which glistened a fair-sized, steep-banked, mountain lake, clogged up with a tangle of weeds. A screaming flock of gulls burst out of the weeds with a series of tiny splashes. As they rose, Kate flung the coil of rope down, and they both flopped onto the bouncy grass to watch the gulls circle and cry above them.

"There always seems to be more sky when you're on a felltop," Kate murmured. "And that private feeling, like it's all yours up here, too."

The grass was prickly and cool through their sweaty T-shirts. Weary legs flopped loosely and relaxed completely.

Suddenly Kate sat up. "Nick . . .?"

From where Nick was lying she looked funny. He could see right up her nostrils. "Mmmm? *What on earth can she want now?* he wondered. Then he remembered. "OK, might as well. We might lose our balance if we have a *full* knapsack with us, climbing." He tried to sound sensible rather than admitting that he was famished, too. Meat-paste and cheese sandwiches, crisp green apples. The gulls swooped and screamed for pieces of bread, which they flung to them. You can't throw very well when you're sitting down. Kate flapped her arms, anyway, when she threw.

"You look like a great big crow flying off between Great Pike and Highbarrow," Nick laughed. From where he sat the two distant fells seemed to cradle her narrow shoulders. "Crow, CROW! CROW!" he yelled, and it echoed back from the surrounding crags: "CROW! Crow, crow . . ."

She threw her loose, black curls over one shoulder as she turned to "dive and peck his eyes out." Soon he had a mouthful of scarlet T-shirt and a great weight of twin sister on his chest. "What's more," he puffed, forcing the thin, sweat-dried cloth out of his mouth with his tongue, "what's more, in those boots you've got legs like a crow's!"

He'd gone too far. Kate rolled over sulkily onto her tummy, pulling gently at a tuft of grass. "Well, at least my hair's shiny like a crow, which is more than you can say for your mess! Mom told me I *deserved* lovely hair 'cause I brush it every night."

She'd broken a big rule by siding with mom like that. "Phooey on mom!" Nick muttered.

They were both on their tummies on the grass now, and for a long time they stayed that way. When Nick and Kate were together like that half of what passed between them didn't actually have to be said. They understood each other so well that their thoughts just sort of

15

flowed between them, and only now and then would they bother to put them into a sentence.

"Why doesn't dad come back then?" Nick said. He adored his dad. Kate knew this. She knew he was tall and handsome and always made them laugh. But he always seemed to like showing Nick how to make things out in the shed on the woodworking bench—things she wasn't allowed to help with. Dad used to make her help mom with peeling vegetables, which was really boring.

"Home's all sissy when dad's not here," Nick went on. "And mom's useless when she tries to do things without dad being around."

"P'haps you ought to help her more! After all, you're a boy, and you remember how dad said: 'Right, Nick, you're the man in the house, now,' just before he left last time?"

There was a pause. Nick knew his dad had said that, but how could he and Kate have this kind of fun if mom was dragged into it? "S'pose you think she should be with us now, then?" he asked. "And s'pose I ought to lead *her* climbing on a crag!" They both had visions of their pasty, unfit mom grappling with a quarry face . . . and both burst out laughing.

Then suddenly Kate was serious, "Nicky? Don't you think . . . we ought to forget the climbing idea for today?"

He was stunned at first. Then he worked out

why she'd said it. Yes, all their plans for the climb, the practicing on an old oak tree right at the bottom corner of the garden . . . it'd all been fun because it gave them a secret, apart from mom. Now—well, they could do what they wanted, anyway, up here. And he was warm, drowsy, lazy. So was Kate.

What's more, he thought, *if we don't use the rope we needn't tear the Co-op tags and then have to explain that away to mom when she wants to use it for her washing.*

He knew Kate could tell by his silence that he sort of agreed with her. She propped herself up on her elbows and gave him a real, Kate smile. She'd been scared about the climbing, he knew, though she'd never have admitted it.

"Let's just lie here until it's time to go down," she said, "then we can look mom straight in the face and tell her exactly what we've done all day. That's honest, isn't it?"

Sometimes Nick got cross with Kate for caring about being honest like that.

"Tell you what, though," he suggested, "how about running the screes on the way down instead? All that debris from the landslides makes great sliding." After all, it'd be a bit chicken to do *nothing* with this whole day they'd got to themselves.

Kate's brown face turned away for a moment. "We won't be able to get a drink from the stream on the way down," she murmured. Then she turned to face him again. He knew she was struggling with her nerve. She'd never chickened out yet. He was better at ball games, she was better at helping old Fred with the garden; but as far as sheer guts went, they'd never failed each other. But could she face plunging down the great scree of loose rocks and boulders?

She nodded without speaking. It was then that, looking down the slope, she saw the little pony. He was grazing by himself about a hundred meters from them. "Look, Nick!" she whispered. "It can't be wild, surely; but look at his tangly mane and how long his tail is."

Nick peered up from where he was lying.

"He's much smaller than Dinah," Kate continued, comparing the little black pony with the old cart horse Tom Fawcett used to haul loads of hay up from his meadows to his farm. She and Nick had spent fun evenings lying on their tummies on top of the hay, gazing down at the old horse's brown rump.

"He's probably some farmer's young colt, up here till he's strong enough to work," Nick remarked. Suddenly he leapt to his feet, waved his arms wildly and yelled, "CROW! CROW!" And as the pony disappeared at a gallop into the bracken the echo came back from the crags: "CROW, crow. . . ."

18

"You've scared him," Kate exclaimed.

"Oh, c'mon. Let's get moving." Nick urged her, feeling energetic now that he was back on his feet. He hauled Kate up by one hand.

Her face was solemn again. "Not scared . . .?" Nick teased.

She closed her eyes and shook her head.

They found a splendid scree, spilling down from the foot of a great, looming cliff. The loose rocks spread out and fell away below them, growing like a spotlight beam till they finally disappeared out of sight.

Nick turned to Kate and smiled, then winked. "C'mon, we'll keep to the side just in case things get out of control! And look, you mustn't get right above me or your rocks might crash into my back. So you start right at the edge, and I'll go just a little way over."

They stepped gingerly out onto the great, gray, jagged mass of boulders, wedged by smaller rocks and sprinkled with loose pebbles that slipped and rattled as they stepped on them.

"At least you've got the right shoes on," Nick admitted, seeing she needed encouragement. "OK then?" Kate was poised, tense and crouching a little, clinging to the bracken shoots growing out onto the edge of the scree. Again she closed her eyes and nodded gently.

"Right. Let's go!"

Despite this brave war cry they both inched forward nervously, moving down as if they were on a slippery stairway . . . almost as if they were both rather scared.

"Look, Crow," Nick stopped, calling her the new nickname he had just given her. "This ain't no fun. In fact we'd have moved faster if we'd raced down through the bracken. To make this work we've got to really *move* and get the scree moving with us so we're on a kind of conveyor belt. C'mon, Crow. This should be next-best to flying once you really get started!"

They both began to trot gently but in fact they weren't moving any faster, just running up and down on the spot. This was daft! Then something wild broke loose inside Nick. "Wow-eeeee!" he yelled, and he flung his legs forward in great, leaping strides, seesawing his arms to hold balance as his feet twisted and fell on the uneven, jagged rocks. His parka flapped wildly around his thighs. He flung his face against the air rising from the valley below. "Wow-eeee!" The scree had begun to shift with the pounding of his feet. Gradually, first with a slow rattle, but soon with a throaty roar, the whole mountainside became a harsh cogwheel beneath his flying feet. His eyeballs bounced with each slap of the gym shoes on hard rock. "Wow-eeeee!"

"Nick!" A panic scream just to his left. Kate.

He'd forgotten about Kate. His knees locked rigid on the boulder he'd landed on. Gradually it slid and wobbled to a halt on the bed of smaller, faster-rolling pebbles beneath it.

In the silence that followed he turned majestically to his left. "Nick, my hand!" The palm of Kate's left hand was dripping with bright crimson blood. Nick watched, his eyes recovering from the jolting and settling, fascinated, on the fierce red drips.

Kate's face was very pale through her tan and looked more big-eyed than ever. Her mouth hung open rather foolishly. She didn't look quite all there. "I grabbed a bracken, Nick, and it cut right through. We were out of control, Nick. I was so scared."

"You were out of control, you mean!" At last, on this scree, he had felt strong and free, like his dad, crashing through rough seas on a minesweeper. Every muscle in his body was tingling. If Kate chose to chicken out at this point, well—hard luck on Kate. Nick turned a smug smile on her. "If you're scared then I'm sorry, Crow," he poised his arms like a glorious eagle, " 'cause I am a real bird!"

And he flung himself on down the scree, his heart thudding, nerves thrilling to feel the pounding, vibrating rock move again. The roar rose to a peak as he swiftly gathered speed and plunged downwards. This, surely, was it! Life, beyond mom, school, even beyond fear itself.

And then, he just—missed his footing. As one ankle crumpled under him he sank onto his hip and the smaller rocks began to pound against his ribs, over his legs. Crouched like this, he slid another hundred meters before crashing to a halt against a slightly larger rock. Every muscle in his body was exploding now, in a panic, twitching and contracting in strange knots and cramps as he lay there. He felt he'd hurtled against some terrible, forbidden barrier. His body was jangling with alarm signals. Then his cheek sank against the cool rock. His eyes closed, and he was held by a gentle, blotting-out numbness until Kate arrived.

"Nick?" A hand was touching his sweat-soaked T-shirt. They stared at each other for a long time. Both of them must have been wildly changed by fright. Kate seemed so ugly! Her face was all heavy and white. She seemed to have lost control over her mouth. It still hung down at one side in that silly way. And then, "Look, Nick! Look at your ankle!" she gasped.

One ankle was slim, straight and brown, the blood pulsing quickly beneath the skin. The other was already a blue-white, swollen lump. He couldn't move it or feel it at all.

"And look where we are!" Kate sobbed, gazing wildly around them. He followed her eyes and what he saw thrust him deeper into his nightmare. That dive had hurled him straight downwards. A long way. Meanwhile the edges of the scree had fanned out away from them till they could barely see them in the distance. They were more or less in the middle now, and, as they'd expected, the scree was even steeper here and plunged on downwards until it became nearly vertical, and disappeared from sight.

Very gently Kate put her arms around Nick. Blood had spattered down her leg from the cut on her hand. For a long time they crouched together and sniffed and whimpered to each other. Then at last Kate rose to her knees and Nick looked up at her. She was still very white, but her face was the right shape again. In fact, it was calm and rather lovely. "Should I go down or across, d'you think!"

"Down. If you go across on the slippery surface the rocks'll move and crack into you from above. You've got to go down, with them."

She was sucking her cheeks in by now but still gazing into his face. There was a flicker of a smile and she rose to her feet.

"*Now* just watch! Now you're going to see how a crow *really* ought to fly!" She turned away.

As she moved off Nick watched her shoulder blades shift with the movement of her arms. Her parka flapped with the staggering movement of her legs as the scree began to slip beneath her. She seemed so unreal, her movements so odd. But she was the only chance he had.

Gradually she became a red and black blob. Then just a red dot as she slipped away down the terrifying slope. Soon she disappeared out of sight altogether because it got even steeper down there.

Nick didn't think about her bravery; his mind was dead, his ankle numb, his body aching and getting stiff. He just felt surprised that Kate had sucked her cheeks and yet not chickened out. Then he realized they'd left the rope up by the small lake, and he wondered how they'd explain it to mom. He settled the floppy pad of the empty knapsack between his cheek and the boulder.

Suddenly he felt he wasn't alone. Looking sideways across the scree to the fellside a long way beyond, he saw the silhouette of the little black pony watching him. He was chest-high in the bracken, but his head was flung high, turned towards him, ears pricked. And very still.

Two

THE MIST WAS THINNING. As Nick gazed up at the white walls around him he saw beady eyes, becoming clearer, more piercing. Yes, they were the bright glass eyes of his stuffed fox's head. There was its sharp nose and the lolling plastic tongue.

That fox! So it had to be his bedroom . . . gradually he became aware of the smoothness of the sheets against his hands and face.

Then a strange sound bored through his grogginess, a heavy drone . . . something grinding up the drive in low gear? He rolled onto his right elbow so that his chin came level with the window ledge. A blue and white Landrover was swinging around in front of the house. He heard the front door open directly beneath him, and soon two figures came slowly out from the house, down the steps leading to the drive. As he was above them he could only see the tops of their heads. Not their legs. They seemed to glide like people in a dream. One had a green and white checked blouse on . . . checked blouse? Mom! The other had the same reddish hair. He couldn't see their faces. They paused—the second lady stretched an arm around mom's shoulders and squeezed her tightly. They moved on. It was all very strange.

The Landrover's doors slapped open together. Three men stepped out, dressed in breeches, boots, and bright shirts. They moved slowly to the back of the Landrover, out of Nick's view, and only the tops of their heads remained in sight over the canvas roof. Mom and the other lady stopped at the bottom of the steps. They were very close to each other and very upright.

The men's heads bobbed in a strange pattern. Mom suddenly twisted her face onto the other lady's shoulder and raised her hands to her eyes. The three men's heads moved together now, keeping the same distance between them. As they inched round the side of the Landrover the reason for this became clear:

they carried between them a long board draped with a blanket that was molded into slight curves by a shape that lay beneath it.

At each end of the board, one man held two poles with stiff, braced arms. It must have been quite heavy. The third, the oldest man, came towards mom and held out his hand. It was Tom Fawcett. Mom took Tom's hand briefly, then crushed her face back onto the other lady's shoulder.

The man's lips were moving. He didn't seem to know where to look. Then they all moved up the steps towards the house, mom and the other lady coming last. The younger man at the back end of the board fumbled with his boots on the pathway, probably he couldn't see where the steps were. As they passed under Nick's window their board was just a navy blue shape. The bumps didn't show from above.

Floorboards creaked down in the hall. A voice was giving short, soft orders. Then a door closed. The dream had melted. There was just a complete silence.

Nick's elbow was stiff, his mind numb. Pictures from the last five minutes lay on his brain, meaningless. He shifted to stretch the stiff arm. The sheets rustled reassuringly. Familiar objects in the room comforted his mind: his scarf on the chair beneath the grinning fox, a tumble of books on the shelf between the chair and the window. He looked at the gleaming wardrobe, at the framed photo of the foxhounds, which dad had given him the Christmas before last. Then back to his scarf on the chair . . .

. . . a square four-walled room: it was a prison! He pushed back the covers and swung his legs violently over the side of the bed and onto the floor.

In the same movement he rocked his weight forward out of the bed, pushing behind him on the pillow.

The next thing he knew, his nose was in the old rag rug, his body skewed sideways on the floor, and a pain was burning in one leg. It must have given way. Everything was quiet again. He lay there because there seemed no point in fighting this nightmare anymore.

Much later the door opened, and he heard two pairs of sandals on the linoleum. They paused. Someone gasped and gave a little moan. Then arms raised him, and he was back on his bed. He focused his eyes slowly on two figures looming over him: the green and white of mom's blouse . . . mom! She was crying softly.

The other lady tucked Nick in again. A Landrover was running quietly down the drive. Landrover? Oh, yes. . . .

"Mom? What's going on? What's happening, mom?"

The other lady answered, "Nick, my love,

just lie there quietly now. You're very safe. Don't you know where you are?"

"Course I do! I'd know that old fox anywhere!"

"And you remember who I am."

"You look like Nige."

"That's right, Nick. I'm your Aunt Meg. Surely you know me? That knock on the head must have made you forgetful. I left Nige at home with Uncle Roger today."

Interesting . . . so that was sorted out.

"What was on that board just now?"

Mom gave a little choke and stopped crying. Nick felt she must be holding her breath. Suddenly everything felt tense, quiet. Aunt Meg had gone solemn and was sitting very upright on the edge of the bed. She was trying to catch mom's eye.

". . . and why a blue and white Landrover? Usually they're green."

This time Aunt Meg was ready. She turned towards him, laid a hand on his knee, and drew a deep breath.

"Nicky, you'll have to know sometime. You've had a nasty accident. Your ankle will be sore because you twisted it badly up on the Castle How screes. Your head probably feels vague and dizzy, because I guess you hit it on rocks; and then spent the night up there with only your T-shirt and shorts. And as you weren't back by sunset Carol ordered out the Mountain Rescue Team."

"Carol? Who's Carol?"

"Oh, I'm sorry, Nick." Aunt Meg was all keyed up for some reason. "I meant to say your mom. She's always been Carol to me because she's my sister—you know that!"

"Mountain Rescue? Ooooh!" Nick was rather impressed by the idea. "But—hey!" Nick suddenly burst out as his mind caught the real meaning of being rescued by the team. "What about Kate? She was the one who was supposed to get you! Why did the Mountain Rescue have to come into it?"

There was another silence. Aunt Meg stood up and put her arm round mom's shoulder. Mom began a choked, terrible sobbing.

"Nick?" Aunt Meg was looking right at him now. "Had you fallen before Kate left you? So she went for help for you?"

He nodded impatiently. Why wouldn't they give him the answer he wanted? "But where *is* Kate?" he pressed.

"Nick . . . Kate is dead." There was an empty pause. Even Nick's fuzzy brain could tell that. Aunt Meg was thinking what she could say next. "When the Mountain Rescue found you, Kate was nowhere nearby so . . ." Aunt Meg was the most peculiar color by now. Nick watched her cheeks. They were like margarine.

"Well," she continued slowly, "Tom and the Mountain Rescue couldn't find Kate anywhere so they asked Bob Dean if he'd take his foxhounds out to search the fellside for her. And they came across her, down beneath that scree somewhere. And just now," she quickened her words as though rushing to finish the sentence in one breath, "the Mountain Rescue Landrover—that was the blue and white one— it's just brought Kate back to us."

"So Kate *is* back and downstairs?"

Aunt Meg's pale cheeks wobbled. "But Nick," she broke in, "you must understand— Kate isn't here any more—she's dead. She's gone to . . . be with Jesus. That's just her old body down there."

Mom by this time was sobbing so hard that she couldn't breathe properly.

"Come on, Carol, let's go and make a pot of tea. It will take a while to recover from a crack on the head like that," Aunt Meg murmured. Together they rose and walked slowly out through the door. Aunt Meg reached back to close it softly and firmly.

Nick lay still, completely still. He wasn't blinking at all. Just staring at his stuffed fox's head grinning at him on the opposite wall . . . he remembered how the fox had become his.

Slowly the scene came back to him: one bleak day the previous winter the foxhounds had killed that fox below Castle How. The twins had just got off the school bus on their way home when the excited hounds came plunging down the fell through the russet bracken on their way back to their kennels. The huntsman, Bob Dean, had presented Nick with the tattered head of the fox, smiling and saying, "That there fox has got through a few hundred hens in its time. Hope you'll come out hunting with us when your legs is a bit longer!" Nick was proud yet horrified by the still-warm bundle in his hand. Mom had been pretty brave when he'd marched into the kitchen with it. She'd had it stuffed as his Christmas present. They'd cleaned it up and put in those shiny, staring glass eyes. He was going to show it to his dad when he came home.

But now as he lay gazing at those cruel glass eyes they seemed to stare right through his own . . . through into his brain. He was staring into the eyes of a killer.

Slowly Nick rose from his bed. He moved very carefully this time; cool yet utterly determined. He laid the covers back in two neat folds, stepped onto the linoleum, and hobbled round the bed, gripping at the bottom to balance himself.

Then he knelt on the chair, and slowly hauled himself up till he was standing firmly on his good foot. Gently, carefully, he reached up and unhooked his fox's face from the wall. Then, holding it under one arm, he sank onto the seat of the chair. Sitting very correctly, his feet flat on the floor, he took the fox in both hands, held it out before him, and stared straight into its murderous glass eyes for a long time.

Suddenly a great roar escaped from somewhere inside him. He pulled at those bits of glass and flung them to the floor. Then he hurled the head through the window pane, smashing the glass noisily.

Everything was silent, except for a startled blowfly who came out from behind the wardrobe. Nick watched him circle, heard his angry buzz.

When Aunt Meg rushed up the stairs to see what was going on, she found him sitting on the edge of his bed, picking pieces of splintered glass from the folds of his sheets. His left thumb was bleeding red spots onto the whiteness, but he wasn't feeling any pain.

* * *

For several days Nick was just a dummy. When he was hungry, Aunt Meg brought him a little blue tray with a bowl of cornflakes or soup on it, and he'd lift the spoon to his mouth, lower it, lift it, lower—like a robot—till his stomach wasn't empty anymore. When he wanted to go to the bathroom, Aunt Meg would help him hobble along the landing. He began to notice that this was getting easier. Soon he could put a little weight on the bandaged foot, less on Aunt Meg. Once or twice the doctor came, unwrapped the tight bandages, felt the stiff, puffy ankle joint with gentle hands, then bandaged it again.

Nick didn't want the radio. He never thought of reading. His mind was numb, except for two occasional thoughts: where was Kate, and when would his dad come? His mind would not take in what had really happened.

One morning Aunt Meg made him get dressed. It took a long time for him to hop and be hoisted from step to step down into the hall and around the kitchen. It gave him time to notice things. They were the same as ever: the grandfather clock, the sun shining through the window in the front door. They didn't go into the porch so he couldn't see if Kate's climbing boots were still there or not.

They turned into the kitchen. Aunt Meg pulled out a chair, sat Nick down, and then took the next one for herself.

"Well, between us we took," she glanced at the kitchen clock, "two and a half minutes . . . not bad for a three-legged race downstairs!" She had lovely brown eyes, and her frizzy red hair escaped in wisps from her bun and formed a hazy crown around her head.

"Where's mom?" Funny—he hadn't realized that she wasn't around till now.

"Out shopping in Moseley . . . she likes doing things by herself at the moment. But finding you up and about'll be a wonderful surprise for her."

"And where's Kate?" Nick broke in. This seemed to take Aunt Meg by surprise.

"Kate's body has been buried behind the church in the village, Nick—but the real Kate—she's . . . gone to be with Jesus."

"Oh—that's all rot!" Aunt Meg jumped and went red. But she didn't argue with him. Instead, she changed the subject.

"Look, Nick, we've decided that you should have a real break. See some different faces, do new things. Now, I'm going to stay here with Carol—your mom—for another week or two. But as far as I can gather on the phone, your Uncle Roger and Nige are getting very fed up with each other's company. So the plan is that you should go over and stay with them—at Ellerthwaite."

She paused. Her brown eyes were watching him closely. He'd heard everything she said perfectly clearly, but he hadn't quite taken it in.

"Mind you, the idea of three menfolk running a house is pretty terrifying!" She laughed and added, "But you'll be able to do all sorts of things together. There's Nige's new bike and plenty to do and see in Moseley . . . and the lake."

Nick wasn't very impressed by this. He couldn't imagine Nige ever letting him near his precious new bike. And what good was a lake when you could never afford to go out in a speedboat? But Aunt Meg's eyes looked almost hurt. He put on a big, silly smile.

"Yeah—that'll be OK!" It'd probably be far from OK. Nige was brainy and also rather fat and lazy. Even Kate had been able to beat him in the hundred meters, and he was a year older than the twins!

* * *

As a house, Ellerthwaite wasn't bad. Uncle Roger was a drilling engineer, and the company he worked with often sent him overseas. He'd brought bits and pieces back with him from the countries he'd been to: long, wooden African masks, horsewhips from South America, bongo drums, carved ivory elephants. Nick had always liked Ellerthwaite. So had Kate. It rained a lot in the Lake District, and there weren't many houses where you could pass wet afternoons in such interesting ways. Nige and the twins had made Red Indian camps in the attic, and hacked at each other with blunted tomahawks. They'd "burnt each other at the stake" and beaten out wild war dances on the bongo drums.

But all this meant that, now, it was so full of memories of Kate.

However, big, friendly Uncle Roger took part of his annual summer holiday for Nick's visit, and over the next few days spent hours telling long, gripping stories about the African jungle, leafing through books with him: picture books about Pacific islands and Arctic icebergs, tropical birds and beautiful Arab horses. Sometimes when he'd gone to fix supper, Nick would take down books about the Himalayan mountains or the Andes and gaze, fascinated, at the towering peaks shooting up into the cold, blue skies. Sometimes he looked up at the slopes, but sometimes he found himself staring down into the precipices. And he went all numb again. He didn't understand why he took these books down, but he knew he couldn't stop himself.

Uncle Roger and Nige were terrific. Everything in that house was Nick's if he wanted it. Nige pushed him along on that new racing bike—up the drive, then he could freewheel back down to the house by himself, resting the bad foot on the pedal. Nige had never let the twins near that bike—ever.

Uncle Roger and Nige had both been working on an enormous jigsaw puzzle in the front hall. When Nick came to stay, they let him join in. They had already done most of the sky and the outside edges—all the boring bits—but they let Nick have the fun of doing the yacht's sails, the details of the rigging, the bright T-shirts of the sailors, and their different faces.

Once Nick came hobbling in from the garden on the crutches the doctor had lent him. It was starting to drizzle outside. Nige was bent over the jigsaw table in the hall. As he heard Nick's sandals and crutches coming across the floorboards, he lifted his head. Nick just caught sight of the quickest scowl of annoyance across Nige's face before he smiled.

"You've turned up just right—I've got stuck on the waves—they all seem the same."

Mmmm, Nick thought. *Think you can kid me with that "just right"! OK—I'll take you up on it . . .!*

"Actually, I *was* going to get my parka, and then go out again," Nick said, and sighed. "But if you're really stuck . . ." He hauled himself in front of the table, spreading the crutches so Nige had to sit on the stairs. From there he could only see the puzzle upside down.

Nick was secretly pleased. He just couldn't see why Nige should enjoy that jigsaw—just as he couldn't see why that fox's head should've grinned . . . grinned . . . grinned. Why should they be so happy, he wanted to know, when he was so miserable? What made things worse was that, even from upside down, Nige was managing to do more of the jigsaw than he was.

Three

NIGE AND UNCLE ROG loved boats as much as Nick did, but they'd never had their own dinghy on the lake. Sometimes, though, Uncle Rog drove the two boys down to Moseley Bay in his old Morris, and they'd all sit on the pier watching the great, white steamers edge in until they bumped against the wooden boards and made the whole pier shudder beneath them. Then sailors in blue sweaters and faded jeans would leap ashore with coils of rope and lash the restless things firmly to iron posts. Gangplanks would be wheeled into position. Finally hordes of wind-blown, chatty vacationers would swarm down onto the pier.

Uncle Rog hadn't the money to take the boys on the steamer, but it was good fun just watching.

When Nige's birthday came on August 24, well, that was different. It was a fabulous day—during breakfast the sun streamed in through the kitchen window. Most likely Nige missed not having his mom there for his birthday, though he didn't show it in front of his dad and Nick.

But Uncle Rog must have known how he must be feeling; that was why he'd decided on a really great present. As the three of them cracked into their boiled eggs he announced it in a very matter-of-fact way. "I was quite surprised to find Ralph Parr has water skis for kids. Wouldn't have thought many could afford it. . . ."

Nige was a bit tubby and pasty. He always took some time to wake up properly in the morning. Nick had been very untalkative since he arrived, anyway. But Uncle Roger could be depended upon to break the breakfast silence with a steady flow of nonsense and useless information (usually about rare and weird African birds).

Now he paused. They were all digging gently into the soft yolks of their eggs, trying not to spill them. "Mind you," he added at last, "Ralph did say he reckoned kids were by far the quickest learners. Hope so, because I certainly can't afford to pour more than half an hour's worth of gas into that thirsty speedboat of his!"

Surprisingly Nige, like lots of tubby, pasty kids, was an excellent swimmer. He'd hardly taken in his dad's first remarks, but he'd heard that last bit all right. "Wow!—fantastic! At last! Ralph Parr . . . Hey, how many tries do I get? As many as I can cram into half an hour?"

Even Nick was excited. "A speedboat!" he shouted with a voice that hardly sounded like his own. He hadn't been enthusiastic about anything since he'd arrived at Ellerthwaite, not since that climb on the fells.

The zippy little boat could only take two so when they got down to the pier Uncle Roger insisted that Nick should go in the boat instead of him. He lowered Nick off the dock into Ralph Parr's strong, brown arms. Nick settled on the damp, plastic seat and tried to understand the dials while Ralph was shouting instructions out over the stern to Nige who was fitting on the skis.

If dad could see me now! Nick was thinking . . . and it made him wonder *why* his dad hadn't come home when he'd heard about . . . the accident . . . perhaps Uncle Roger would know? Nick decided he must remember to ask when they got back.

At last Ralph turned, and shoved the throttle

forward. The low pulse of the engine rose to a roar. The needle on the speedometer jerked up. The stern of the boat sank into the water as the bows rose, and she pounced forward. There was a sharp tug on her as the towrope tautened, and she began to haul Nigel out of the lake. He'd been waist deep but now rose slowly, slowly, behind his own great bow waves until his square, white body was high above the water, the rope so tight that a row of glistening drops was jerked off it.

The most enormous grin sliced across his round, white face. His eyes were closed tightly against the spray. The wind whipped his red hair so hard that it seemed to have been blown off the back of his head.

Ralph braced his arms against the wheel, set the little boat on a course towards the center of the lake, and it scudded out, the hull slapping rhythmically across the top of the tiny waves.

"He's a good sportsman!" Ralph shouted over the roar of the outboard. Nige was balancing beautifully, curving his skis a little to one side and then to the other as he became more sure of himself.

"Funny, really, he's not got a likely build to his body, I'd say you'd be more the type to make a good skier. Bit more athletic!"

Just what Nick had been thinking . . . if fat old Nige could do it, well, he could've shown them.

"I suppose," Ralph shouted again, "you did your ankle in on something much more exciting, eh?"

He looked across at Nick, waiting for a reply. The sun sparkled on the water as it streaked past. The now-distant shore was being wound along as if it were on a filmstrip. Sea gulls dived dizzily above them. The boat sprinted on wildly. The pulse of the waves beat on her hull.

"Accident, was it?" Ralph bawled.

Nick was trapped, imprisoned on this vast stretch of open water, caught in the whirlpool of movement and speed. He shut his eyes tightly, and gripped the seat. The roar of the outboard filled his brain, and he couldn't escape the vibration of the boat racing beneath him.

He locked every muscle he had, trying to barricade himself against the speed, against the brilliance of sun and water—against the directness of Ralph's question. He closed his eyes tighter—but pictures started to form on the darkness of his eyelids. He saw bracken, sky, and fells swirling round him. His legs were vibrating, not on the scudding waves now, but on the downward tumble of sliding stones. The roar of the outboard motor became the roar of the Castle How scree.

He opened his mouth to scream, but it was filled with a spray of cold lake water. The shock was such that he closed his mouth and gulped while in his mind the scree rush plummeted him on down the fellside.

Suddenly an angry shout from Ralph broke into his nightmare. "Watch it! Changing course like that. . . ."

Nick's eyes jerked open. One of the enormous lake steamers was cruising away just ahead of them. They were scudding straight for its spreading wake. Within seconds their boat was pounding awkwardly across the giant waves, bucking in the air like an injured antelope. Nick's grip shifted and tightened on the side of the boat. His stomach heaved. Ralph's right hand wrestled with the kicking wheel. His left arm—hard as a boulder—crashed against Nick's stomach and pinned him to the back of the seat to prevent him from being flung out into the water.

The instant they were clear of the steamer's wake, they both twisted to watch Nige. His skis hit the first waves, and he shot into the air.

"Let go! Let go!" yelled Ralph as he cut the engine. But Nige's arms were still strained forward onto the tow bar. He landed and bounced up again. The skis were crossed now, his left shoulder towards the boat. When he landed again, he fell into the waves, his body sending up a great spurt of brilliant spray as it was dragged along.

44

The boat cruised to a halt. The race of water settled to a gentle slap-slapping in a terrible, overwhelming silence. The distant fells were still, the lake oval and steady around them. Nick was drenched. When he licked his upper lip, it was salty with sweat that had been blown right across his cheeks. His bare back came noisily away from the plastic seat. Again, the stickiness was sweat. And yet it was very cool out there on the lake.

Nige was thrashing around awkwardly in the water. The skis jerked up at odd angles as he struggled to get free of them. Ralph coaxed a gentle chug-chug from his boat before turning her round towards Nige.

They drifted up to him sideways. The skis were floating on the surface by now, like driftwood. Nige's round face was white and empty-looking on the surface of the water like a head without a body.

Ralph hauled him up over the side of the boat. It rocked over with his weight. Then his squirming body was between Nick and Ralph on the seat, and his cold, white arm was rubbing against Nick's brown, sweaty one.

All the way back to the wharf, Nige chattered away at the top of his voice. Ralph was still cursing at the steamer. They weren't really talking to each other, just shouting, separately, into the breeze, both rather excited. So neither of them noticed that Nick wasn't saying a thing.

As they drew nearer to the wharf Uncle Roger's large figure became more distinct. Soon Nige was beside him on the planking, struggling into his navy sweater and carrying on in the same, high voice. The whole way back in the car he never stopped, still shouting as if he was out in the middle of the lake.

* * *

Somehow, in all the last minute rush before going to stay with her sister, Aunt Meg had managed to bake a beautiful white-iced cake, which she had hidden high on a shelf in the pantry. As soon as Nick and Nige had brushed their wet hair and sat down at the kitchen table Uncle Roger appeared with the magnificent thing. Nige squawked with excitement. He was obviously ravenous after the waterskiing. And he must have been afraid there wouldn't be a cake this year. The thirteen flickering candles didn't show up very well as the sun was still so bright, but he stood up very solemnly and leaned forward over the table to blow them out.

Nick watched him numbly, remembering cakes he and Kate had shared. Their birthday was in January, and mom had always done great snow scenes in white icing on top of their cake. Kate had pink candles and Nick's had been blue. And he'd always been cross that she was allowed to blow hers out first because she was the girl . . . and he'd got really annoyed if she'd blown any of his out by mistake.

Now Nige was slicing into his own great, white cake with the gleaming carving knife. Very deliberately, with a wide, fixed grin on his face.

Suddenly it all hit Nick at once: that grin was like the fox's crazy sneer. He heard the crunch of the knife through the hard white icing and heard Kate's huge boots in the scree. Suddenly there was no one, nothing left anywhere, in all the world, for him . . . she had gone.

Tears came rushing up into his eyes and flowed out onto his face. He started crying like a baby, sobbing and choking until he could hardly catch his breath. He buried his head on his arm as it lay stretched along the edge of the kitchen table and, for the first time since the accident, really wept with all he had.

Uncle Roger helped him upstairs and into the little bedroom at the back of the house, which had been his since he arrived. It was easier to cry on the bed. Uncle Roger stayed with him, just a hand on his shoulder, until he'd wept himself to exhaustion.

Then Nick rolled over and looked straight at his uncle. There was nothing else left to do.

"Don't worry, Nick. I thought you'd have a good cry, sometime. Now it's all come out at once."

"Sorry, though," Nick swallowed, "after all, it's Nige's birthday." To be honest, he was still feeling bad towards Nige. It was the way he had skied so well, and then had gone on about it all the way home in the car. It was his smug, grinning face. He'd been having a great time, but all the while his fun had meant this buildup of misery for Nick.

Uncle Roger looked solid, sitting on the edge of the bed. He had an orange toweling shirt on, soft and friendly.

"Don't worry about it being Nige's birthday, Nick. I can only guess what you must be going through."

Nick suddenly realized how sick he was of keeping all his horror and his anger bottled up inside himself. And when Uncle Rog spoke like that he wanted to tell him about it . . . he must tell him, or he'd burst.

First he told Uncle Rog about the waterskiing: about how it had reminded him of the scree, about the speed and the dizzying movement of the fells around them, about the nightmare that had swamped him when he'd closed his eyes, the thrashing skis, Nige's head like a ball bobbing on the water, a head without a body. Finally he tried to explain the scrunch of the knife going into that cake.

As he was talking, he didn't look at the big, friendly man beside him. He was trying to be

really truthful and that meant somehow looking inside himself.

When Nick finally ran out of story, he did
look at his uncle—suddenly afraid of how he'd
taken it all. He saw he was very still, very serious, gazing at him. Nick realized that he had
probably been like that all the time, and he felt
a bit stupid. "Sorry," he mumbled, wondering
whether it had been a big mistake to say anything at all.

"Don't be crazy!" Uncle Rog butted in, smiling. "No, what I mean is, you're not crazy,
Nick." He became serious again. "I can see
what it's all about now. But what you've got to
realize is that a lot of this terror is just in your
head. Look at it this way: the last person who
was scared out there on the lake was Nigel! And
he was the one who perhaps should have been.
Ralph was just hopping mad and tends to swear
a bit. All you had to do was to sit like a sack of
potatoes. Then we come back here and Nige
gets a whopping great birthday cake for his tea.
Now, think about it that way, Nick, and it
doesn't seem so bad, eh?"

Nick looked steadily at his uncle's friendly
face, hardly hearing what he was saying, just
watching every normal, affectionate expres-
sion of his mouth, his kind eyes.

Yes, he could trust Uncle Roger. "But what
about Kate?" he burst out.

"Kate?" Uncle Rog repeated gently. He wasn't shocked by the question. But he took his time in finding the right answer.

"Well, Kate's fine—just fine . . ." Nick waited, breath held. He knew Uncle Roger wouldn't just palm him off with some sentimental rubbish. "Kate was only young, that's almost the worst thing. Because most people don't die till they're old and crotchety. But she was a dear girl . . ." Now Uncle Rog looked away out of the window for a moment. Nick guessed that perhaps he was close to crying, himself.

As he waited, though, he felt a stab of pain inside as he remembered how he and that "dear girl" had sometimes cheated their uncle. Like the time they'd left a wooden African mask out in the bamboo canes during a thunderstorm and later buried it so he'd never find out.

Uncle Rog turned to him again, his face calm. "She was a dear girl, Nick, but we're not perfect, and Jesus knows that. I mean, he was a boy once, too, and went through all the same temptations—to swipe food, tell fibs, show off—the lot. But he does expect us to try . . . to *want* to please him."

"But what's all that got to do with Kate?" Nick interrupted almost angrily. He always got bored when Uncle Rog or Aunt Meg started talking about God and Jesus.

"Just that I know Kate felt Jesus was her special friend. She used to talk about him a lot with Aunt Meg when you boys were out in the woods. He was her most special friend, the one she most wanted to please. And now, of course, she's gone to be with him. Just think how she'll feel about that! The only tragedy—from our point of view—is that she went so soon, and she was so terribly young." He stood up suddenly and walked to the window.

Nick felt quite a lot better, and it was fairly easy to say what came next. "But Kate died because I teased her about being chicken, Uncle Rog. And she really died because she'd gone to get help for me."

Uncle Roger smiled and nodded. There was a long pause, then, "Yes, I know . . . but you've got to admit, Kate's all right, now, eh?" His voice was gentle. Nick nodded dumbly. "So you, in fact, are the problem!" Uncle Rog continued. "We can't have you flinging foxes' heads through windows or bursting into tears every time you go to a birthday party." They both laughed. "No, those things'll wear off in time. In fact . . ." he looked challenging, "what d'you bet we'll have you walking on the high fells again before the end of the year?"

Nick stared at him. His uncle didn't understand, after all. He could never, never walk through the boulders and bracken again!

"Just you believe me!" Uncle Rog smiled.

"But it's all so horrible!" Nick cried. "I mean, even the kids at school will know. And how can I face mom?"

"Ah, but it's Jesus you've really got to worry about, Nick. He's the one that matters. If you could face him, you'd find he would help you face yourself, and everyone else as well."

Nick stared. *Face him? How on earth . . .?*

"Dad!" That was Nige's voice on the stairs. "Dad! There's a couple of sheep in the garden and I can't get them out. They're smashing around in the flower bed. I've been chasing them for ages!"

"Right—coming!" Uncle Rog yelled. Then he turned to Nick. "Well, at least he hasn't been eating birthday cake ever since we came up here!"

Four

NICK COULD NEVER bring himself to the point of saying "Sorry" to Nige for spoiling his tea, but he did try to be nicer to him during that last week he was at Ellerthwaite. In fact he found he didn't have to try. He'd begun to see that there was more to Nige than just a pasty face. And Uncle Rog had talked sense. If somewhere, somehow, there was that great, important Jesus, who was alive and cared about him, Nick, besides having Kate safe with him, maybe there was a reason for living.

Nick's foot was getting much better. He didn't need the old wooden crutches anymore, so neither Uncle Rog nor Nige had to drop what they were doing every time he wanted help going up and down stairs. He could even take his turn on the uphill tramps pushing the bike, and let Nige have his share of rides back down to the house again.

Uncle Rog had mentioned that Aunt Meg was coming back on Saturday, and Nick knew school began on Monday, so he guessed he'd be going back to mom for that last weekend. But he didn't want to think about that, so he didn't.

Very soon, though, Saturday afternoon arrived, and Uncle Roger was backing the old Morris out of the garage. Nige had to swim in the Moseley swimming meet later that afternoon so he was not coming with them. He'd been going on about it all through breakfast. Oh yes, he reckoned breast stroke *was* his best. But Colin Stokes would take a bit of beating. Colin was a big, rough boy in Nick's class at school. Nick really wanted Nige to win. "Tell you all about it on Monday at school!" Nige yelled after them as the car spluttered away down the drive.

So it wasn't until they were on the way that Nick really faced up to the fact that he was going home, and would have to see mom—live with her, in fact.

"How do you feel about it, then?" Uncle Rog asked as they puttered round the lake.

"Dunno, really. It's funny, but for the first time ever I'm quite looking forward to being back at school!" Maybe that had something to do with escaping from mom, and from the house, empty without Kate. But they both laughed.

"Mmm," Uncle Rog added, "but you mustn't let yourself run away from problems, Nick. I mean, you do realize the kids may not be too kind at school. As you said yourself, they're bound to know what's happened."

Nick had managed not to think too much about that. He didn't want to. "Any idea how mom is?" he asked politely.

"Oh, all right, all right. Aunt Meg was on the phone last night after you had gone to bed. But your mom has a way of feeling very strongly about things, you know. And she's bound to feel really bad still about . . . well, about the reasons why Kate died. What you've got to do is make her *want* to forgive you. Make her want to ask God's help to forgive you. But it won't be easy," he sighed, "because she's not a lady who talks easily to God, anyway."

"Why hasn't dad come back?" Nick asked suddenly.

Uncle Rog looked across at his passenger with a serious face. "He wanted to, Nick. But he sent a telegram saying there was a very tricky political situation out there, and as captain of his ship, he just couldn't leave at a moment's notice. I'm sure he'll be home as soon as he can, though. So, until then, Nick, you've got to be the man in the house. You've got to love your mom and help her keep going. . . ."

That was just how his dad had put it when he left . . . you're a man in the house now . . . and that was just what Kate had reminded him, that last afternoon up on the felltop.

They drove on in silence. Nick found himself trying to remember his bedroom, his favorite corners in the garden . . . *their* favorite corners. Everytime he imagined a bush or a tree, Kate was crouching in it. The games he thought of were all the games they'd invented together. And how could you play games alone?

As they turned into the drive Uncle Roger thrust the gear lever forward, and they ground up the steep slope towards the house. Mom's face bobbed into sight at the big front window. She was sitting on the window seat waiting for them. By the time they swept round by the steps, the front door had opened. She and Aunt Meg stood framed in the doorway, and then they came down to welcome them. Nick found himself remembering that day the Mountain Rescue Landrover had come, and the two ladies had moved slowly down the steps—like this—to meet it.

But already that was a dream . . . this was

much more real, and he felt he was himself, strong and normal again. He leapt out of the car, and hobbled as quickly as he could towards them. Mom hugged him, so did Aunt Meg. Nick had never liked being cuddled like this, especially when Kate had been around. He'd thought it was sissy. But this time . . . anything to make things easier.

They stood and chatted on the steps for a while. Neither Nick nor mom did much talking. He noticed her eyes were red and she'd gotten very thin. Aunt Meg was asking whether Nige had been able to find a clean towel in the linen cupboard for the swimming meet.

Eventually Aunt Meg disappeared into the hall to collect her suitcase. She and Uncle Rog kissed Nick and Mom good-bye very fondly. Both women cried a bit. Nick was embarrassed. Then the car doors slammed, and the old Morris was creeping off down the steep drive.

"You seem to have had a good time, anyway, Nick," mom said brightly as she closed the front door behind them.

This one surprised him, and he hesitated. He'd wanted to be honest with her from the start. He'd had a good time, yes, but not just because of the bike and the books and all the other fun they'd had. He had wanted to tell her straight away how Uncle Rog had talked about Kate being with Jesus. But he felt embarrassed.

As he paused he saw she was looking at him anxiously, longing for him to say something.

"Oh, fantastic, mom! Uncle Rog's been great, and I didn't fight much at all with Nige . . . after—after the first few days. In fact he's a really good water-skier."

"You've been waterskiing, have you?"

Nick found it easy to tell her about the great steamer, and Nige being thrown around on his skis like a Ping-Pong ball. He left out the bit about cutting the cake, though. He just went straight on to tell her about the sheep in Aunt Meg's best flower bed.

"But didn't you have some sort of birthday tea?" she asked as they settled down at the kitchen table themselves. Nick fumbled for a bun then took a deep sip of orange drink. He realized Aunt Meg had probably told mom she'd left a cake in the pantry for Nige.

He looked straight at her and replied, "Oh yes! Fabulous cake, too!" How he hated the way mom was asking questions that made him lie! After all, he really had wanted to be honest, to try, at least.

"And I bet Nige wasn't the only pig, if I know you!" She laughed. Nick realized he was taking another bun only because it gave him something to do. Again, she'd cornered him. He knew no one could say he'd been a pig at Nige's birthday tea.

"Oh," he tried to sound relaxed. "I didn't have as much cake as Nigel!" That was true, wasn't it? Then he had a good idea. "Aunt Meg's a super cook, though—and making the cake in such a hurry, too." He hoped that being nice about Aunt Meg would cover up for the fact that he'd more or less told a fib about the cake. But he still felt gnawed up inside. He'd never dreamt it would be so terrible being back with mom.

"Yes," mom sighed, "Aunt Meg's been a dear to me, too." She looked sad again. Nick suddenly understood that she was probably torn up inside, too. But he didn't know what to do about it.

As she washed up the tea things Nick stayed at the table, watching her curved back, wanting to hug her. It was only as she finished that he realized he should have offered to help. He'd just never thought. Never mind. Over this weekend he would try to be really strong. He would even offer to tidy up Kate's room.

"Just going out to weed the parsley," mom said at last, untying her apron. She seemed glad to be going out, away from him.

Nick walked slowly upstairs, gripping the banister to help his weak ankle. He wanted to sneak into Kate's room before he told mom what he was prepared to do.

But the little linoleum-floored room was already completely empty, except for the bed, which had been taken apart and leaned against the wall with a white sheet over it. The curtains had gone. There were just a few wooden rings left on the curtain rail.

Perhaps he should go down and say, "Oh, I see you've done Kate's room already? I was going to offer to help." But he couldn't. The shock of being in Kate's empty room made him feel sick. He remembered the times they'd bounced on that bed till the springs squealed in agony. Then there was that cracked window-pane where he'd tried to throw a cricket ball up to her last summer. Soon he was sobbing again, choking, partly with anger. He'd so wanted to tidy this room for mom, and to do it for Kate, too. Now there was nothing.

He limped through to his own room, flung his clothes off, and was in bed in a minute. The birds were still singing; it was a glorious late-summer evening outside. Nick buried his head under the pillow to shut out the sunshine and the birds. If only he could shut everything else out!

Breakfast, the next morning, was terrible. When dad was at home it was always he who did all the talking . . . and laughing . . . and he made them laugh, too. When he was away it had been the twins who made the noise, with mom quietly concentrating on dishing up the food, clearing plates. Now Nick and mom had to sit opposite each other, and every time Nick looked up from his plate he knew he'd catch her eye, watching him, and have to think of something to say. So he ate with his nose buried in his food.

At Sunday lunch she couldn't stand it any longer. "For goodness sake, sit up, Nicky! You're like a sack of potatoes—and you've actually got gravy on the end of your nose!"

So he had to sit up, had to catch her eye. He couldn't think of anything to say and neither could she. It was so painful that he refused a second helping of trifle and didn't offer to help with the washing up, either—anything to get out of the kitchen!

He loafed around in the garden most of the morning and afternoon. He couldn't face going on the fell.

He soon discovered Kate's boots weren't on the porch, after all. His were there . . . dusty, unused since his father had gone away. There was just a white length of shelf where Kate's had been, dusty round the shape where the two boots had stood.

By Sunday night, Nick really was longing for the first day of school.

Five

"BE DOWN FOR BREAKFAST in three minutes, Nicky, or you'll miss the bus." The Braithwaites always slept late on vacation so it was a shock to be awakened at seven on Monday morning.

Blue trousers, a brown shirt, navy blue tie . . . all unbelievably clean and fresh. Mom had even managed to get last term's egg stains off his tie. Nice to be in long trousers again. Perhaps the kids wouldn't notice his ankle and ask questions . . . he could almost walk without a limp now.

His tanned wrists looked good coming out of the brown shirt cuffs. In fact rather too much arm was showing; he must have grown over the holidays. He'd be one of the tallest in his year, now, just a bit smaller than that great lout, Colin Stokes. He was bound to play for the school junior team at football once his ankle was strong. Yes, he was looking forward to school all right. And it wasn't just a case of running away from mom.

She'd always believed in giving the twins a good breakfast before school: bacon, egg, three slices of toast. She made her own bread when dad was at home, but couldn't bring herself to bother when he was away.

Nick felt really great as he waited at the bottom of the drive for the bus, with a good three minutes to spare. He tipped his cap at a couple of scraggy crows perched on the wall opposite where he was standing. They were glossy and gawky. But Nick was so cheerful about school it didn't really hit him they were . . . crows.

The bus appeared around the bend right on time. Nick climbed aboard, five pence ready. "Mornin', Nicholas," nodded Ken, the driver, as he took the coin. "And Katie—couldn't she face the first day of school then, bless 'er 'eart?"

The shock cut through Nick like a knife. The engine throbbed on, just the same—but inside him there seemed to be an almighty crash. He moved straight on into the bus past the surprised Ken, heading automatically for the third seat back where both twins used to sit together.

The bus moved off. Nick watched the two crows flap lazily away over the wall, and he realized they were crows. The seat beside him remained empty as they stopped for the odd farmer's wife, going shopping, and other schoolchildren.

By the time they'd reached the village, Nick was feeling as limp as an empty knapsack. Ken's harmless joke had hit him like a boulder. He knew now that school was to be pure misery.

Other kids were drifting in. The little iron gate of the playground clanged as they arrived in twos and threes chatting happily and shouting to each other across the yard. Luckily, as Nick walked across from the bus stop, Uncle Roger's car rattled round the corner. Nige— like Colin Stokes—should really have gone to the big Comprehensive in Moseley but it was filled, so for three years the extras had been coming out to the Valley Secondary School.

"Hi! Nige!" Nick shouted, his cheery voice sounding as though it wasn't quite his own. He walked over to the car as it drew up. "Did you win the breast stroke on Saturday?"

"You bet I did! Beat Colin Stokes by three meters, too!"

Uncle Rog leaned across the passenger seat as Nige climbed out. "Good to see you, Nick— and sounding pretty cheerful, too! Keep it up!" He gave a hefty wink, a wave, and was off.

He'd been the only one who'd understood . . . now Nick knew he'd fooled him, too. Because the last thing he really felt like was facing the other kids right now.

Good old Nige helped. He gabbed the whole way—through the iron gate, across the yard, and into the cloakroom. Kate's peg was next to Nick's and it was empty. Then the bell went for assembly, and they were herded in silence into the hall before Nick had time to think.

He'd always shared a desk with Kate. Again, her half was empty. The whole class of twenty-five (no, of course it was twenty-four now) was the same as the term before. Only difference was they were form 2 now, not form 1. So they didn't have pretty Miss Newton for form teacher but ancient Mr. Pratt instead. Mr. Pratt would be taking them for all their English and religious education as well.

The roll was always called as soon as they got to their classrooms. "Askham?"—"Yes, sir." "Bell?"—"Yes, Miss" (Tony Bell acting the fool, pretending he'd forgotten it wasn't Miss Newton anymore). Giggles. Pause. All eyes on Mr. Pratt. "Bell?" he repeated. "Yes, sir." That dealt with Tony. "Braithwaite?"—"Yes, sir." Nick answered.

"Braithwaite?" Mr. Pratt repeated.

Hadn't he heard?

Nick suddenly realized with horror that

they'd forgotten to cut Kate's name out of the class roll from last term . . . but surely Mr. Pratt knew? Nick's mind worked fast. All eyes were on him. It was a kind of struggle for survival. He fought back tears. "Er—I said 'Yes,' sir."

Mr. Pratt looked up—either remembered or saw the empty seat. He looked very upset, and peered at Nick over his half-moon specs. "Sorry, Nicholas—I didn't mean . . ." Then he got confused, looked down, and decided to carry on. "Er—Hodgson?"

The class shuffled with relief as the awkwardness passed. But Nick knew he'd been the cause of it. He'd made them all think. Had they been told already, somehow?

Lessons had never been hard for him. He was clever enough, never worked himself too hard but knew how to do just enough to keep himself out of trouble. He'd been able to help Kate with her math when Miss Newton wasn't watching, and she'd helped him with his spelling. He thrust his head down, rummaging for the books for the coming geography lesson.

As soon as the bell went for break Nick dived out of the room, although nobody in that class was probably less keen to get outside. But he had a plan: it meant he was first into the yard and could spot Nige's red hair easily. When he appeared, Nick headed straight for him. They didn't usually spend time together at school, but luckily, today, a whole crowd was gathering round him to hear about the swimming meet, so Nick mixed in with them and nobody really noticed him.

When the bell rang, they separated toward their different classrooms again. And Nick, in the push in the corridor, found himself shoved up against the boy he most wanted to avoid . . . Colin Stokes, the boy Nige had beaten. He guessed Colin would be the one to enjoy spreading the story about him and Kate. Who could blame him? It must be one of the best stories round!

"So we're spending break with third-years, eh?" he sneered now.

Nick lashed back like a hurt animal. "Just happen to like winners, not losers, for my friends! Three whole meters, wasn't it?"

"You've got nerve!" Colin glared and swore, and went on almost without thinking, "Real nerve for a . . . murderer!"

Nick backed away from him to his seat, stunned. Mr. Pratt was calling for order, trying to quiet the general din. He couldn't have heard anything the two boys had said, but he must have seen it all, and sensed trouble.

"Settle down, settle down. You're all much too excited for an English lesson," he shouted. "I was going to start a new project today, but I think a good, interesting essay to get you down to work would be a better idea. Let's see, let's see . . ." He stared at the ceiling, as though trying to think up a good title quickly.

"Right," he announced. "In your exercise books. 'Mountain Rescue'."

They were all fairly keen on essays. Scuffling, they groped for English books and pens. Then silence.

But Nick was completely numb again. "Mountain Rescue"! Surely it was just a terrible mistake. How could Mr. Pratt expect him to do that?

As all the others lowered their heads Nick stared straight at the old teacher. He caught his eye, and immediately Mr. Pratt's mouth opened to tell him to get on with it. Then he seemed to realize . . . lowered his eyes, ran bony fingers slowly through his thin, gray hair. Nick supposed this to mean that he needn't do the essay. Mr. Pratt wasn't going to make a fuss. But what was he supposed to do with the next half hour, then? He picked up his pencil and laid an arm along his desk top, then, as though he was thinking hard, squashed his face down on his arm, until little red demons danced on his eyelids.

Six

NICK FELT HIS WHOLE LIFE was a great, pus-filled lump, and now the pus was oozing up to the surface of his skin so that everyone could see it. And he felt that the Jesus who was a friend of Uncle Rog and Kate was nowhere near him. Maybe it was all a fairy tale, anyway.

As if it wasn't bad enough to have lost his Kate, home had become unbearable, and even fun like waterskiing had been a torture. And now thirteen weeks of school term stretched ahead of him like an endless nightmare.

Crouched over his desk, he tried to shut out all the hurtfulness around him . . . was this "life"? Was this what he had to face? In which case, perhaps Kate was the lucky one.

Somehow he got through the rest of the day. It was a slight relief at last to escape from the school at the final bell. But standing apart from the others at the bus stop and sitting alone in the third seat back were misery again.

Mom wasn't around when he crept in through the back door. But he went up to his room all the same. He wanted to be alone: just himself—Nicky. No one else. No stares, no snickering, no sly, sideways looks or embarrassing silences. Surely "just Nicky" could find something of that happy life he'd known?

He sat wearily on his bed, looked down at himself and sighed deeply. He was almost too perfect—clean clothes, shining sandals, and skin smooth and brown after the summer. That started him thinking. In any other year there'd have been those little rows of beady scabs, scratching, and itchings across the late-summer tan . . . blackberries!

Memories of long, golden evenings with Kate flooded back. Kate with a purple mouth, tearing her T-shirt on the spikey strands of bramble as she reached for the highest, fattest berries. Kate laughing as her bag bulged faster than his own. Kate dropping her sticky bag on the gritty path as she jumped down from the top of the bank.

It wouldn't be the same . . . but Nick felt that he must not keep on giving in to these memories.

He heard mom downstairs, coming in from the garden. He went down for tea. It seemed that she, like Nick, had made up her mind to talk politely right through tea. He told her who'd moved up, what he thought of Mr. Pratt, and, of course, news of Nige's victory in the swimming meet. But he didn't tell her the important, hurtful bits. None of it. So what he did say seemed a waste of time and almost like fibbing.

As he helped carry the crumby plates and cold teapot over to the sink he finally announced in a firm voice, "I'll be back by seven, mom—just going out for a walk." She turned to him, her forehead worried. He put on his nice-little-surprise-coming smile and promised, "It'll be OK, mom—you wait and see!" But she still looked unsure.

Nick found a plastic supermarket bag in the front porch behind the climbing boots. He slipped quietly through the door and ran lopsidedly down the rough grass to the road. It was a fabulous September evening, soft—almost hazy. And very still. The surrounding fells rested in the golden light, silent and friendly.

The best blackberries always grew along the banks of the brook running along the bottom of the valley. Nick tried racing down the fields, but the uneven clumps of grass turned his ankle and made it hurt, so he jogged instead, holding the bag out behind him like a small, fat parachute.

The berries were at their best, glistening and heavy. Soon he was picking furiously, wishing he'd changed into some old clothes, trying not to rub pricked and purple fingers down the front of his brown school shirt. This was better. He was out of the house, doing something useful. It would take mom ages to brew this lot into jelly! Help to keep her busy, and happy too. School? Oh, forget it! Nobody could spoil this, now.

Oh—no!

Heavy footsteps were approaching, thud-swish, thud-swish through the long, dry grass. Nick swore at the intruder under his breath, stopped picking, and looked up. Ah—it was only Tom Fawcett . . . his tall figure stooped and waving as he strode through the grass. Behind him Gip, his sheep dog, zigzagged, low and swift.

Oh, Tom was all right . . . Nick and Kate had had such good times with Tom. They saw each other at exactly the same moment.

"Well, Nick m'lad, is pinchin' me best blackberries?" Nick knew Tom never really minded them taking his blackberries, always said he reckoned they made up for it by all their help at haytime. "It'll be a good year," he decided, fingering the firm berries.

Suddenly Nick remembered that Tom, of course, was leader of the Mountain Rescue team. Tom had been with them when they brought Kate down. But had he heard the rest of the story? Why Kate had been on the scree? Did he know that Nicky Braithwaite was no better than a murderer?

Nick watched Tom's face carefully as he peered into the bag. But all the lines and wrinkles and muscles were curving now in delight at the fruit. Hard to see if there were any other feelings there.

"Had a good hay crop this year?" Nick wanted to keep the old man with him. He'd come from nowhere, accused him of nothing worse than taking blackberries, and Nick was suddenly afraid he'd melt back into the golden haze of the evening.

"Alreet, alreet, though very late," he nodded. "Shame you couldn't have helped us."

"Couldn't . . .?" Something had prevented him this year. He'd been at Ellerthwaite. Their eyes met quickly. Then Tom straightened up.

"Look, lad, I've got a little colt up on the fellside. I want him down and quieted a bit before winter sets in. Could do with a young pair of legs like yours to help me—frisky little blighter he is, too. Be round tomorrow 'bout this time, eh?"

The tension eased. Nick grinned. That was fantastic. Since his dad's boat wasn't around for him to play on, a young colt would do. The only horse he'd ever been near was Tom's old Dinah. And the roundup would give him an excuse for escaping from home again tomorrow. After all, he couldn't pick blackberries forever.

School the next day was no better, no worse. Nick realized that it would stay that way. Nice kids didn't know what to say to him. And the nasty ones didn't want to speak. Some just snickered and whispered to each other when he was around. He could imagine how the stories were growing behind his back—wild, exaggerated, horrible stories, thanks mostly to Colin Stokes.

But Nick hardly noticed the hard stares in the yard at morning break that day. All break he was dreaming of a wild-eyed black colt. All fell ponies, he knew, were black. Kate had told him. He saw it trotting across the slopes, tail blown out behind—even though there wasn't a breath of a breeze that day!

By lunchtime he saw himself skimming behind the colt across the fellside, swift and clever as Gip, edging him down towards Tom's farmhouse.

Then, as he shuffled along with the line fil-

ing back into the classroom after lunch, a dim
memory crept up on him. He tried to see the
picture more clearly . . . then he knew. He'd
already seen Tom's little colt. He remembered
its pricked ears and high-held head turned towards him across the scree. And he groaned.
Would he never, ever be free of that day?

Evening came at last. But the dried mud of
Tom's farmyard was no place for dreams. As
Nick stood there, waiting for Tom to fetch Gip
from one of the sheds, his mind was clouded
with new worries. What, he wondered, would
he do if the ankle couldn't take the fell slope?

Luckily Tom climbed like all good
shepherds—slowly, steadily, and wasting no
breath on talking. Nick followed close behind
him so that he wouldn't notice the limp or any
pain on Nick's face when an awkward stone
turned his ankle.

Gip, way ahead, found their quarry. The colt
was almost buried in the high brackens, his
head bent through them to the sweet grass
beneath. He heard the swish of brackens, shot
his head high into the air, and stood, alert and
suspicious, just as he'd stood before. His long,
black tail was spread out on the brackens. He'd
probably been swishing flies with it.

Green leaves had got caught in the rough
hair of his mane, giving him a wild and comical
look.

"We'll bring him down right slowly, Nick. If we once start 'im runnin', we won't stand a chance."

Nick nodded wisely, squashing those painful memories that crowded his mind. He leaned his chest into the shoulder-high brackens, and shoved forward a few steps.

"All done by kindness," muttered Tom as Gip slunk away to edge the colt down from the far side, while the two of them stood their ground, ready to cut him off if he tried to escape in their direction.

It would have been great to see him stampede down the rough slope, his coarse black tail streaming out behind him. Tom had told the twins once how the mountain ponies are as sure-footed as goats. But Nick, for one, was in no hurry to send any creature hurtling down a steep fellside. His ankle was stiff, too, from last evening's climb back up to the house with the blackberries. Now he could feel a dull, thick pain, especially if he stepped down the slope onto his ankle. It was all he could do to match Tom's swinging stride and listen to his admiring comments as he pointed out, with his stick, what a bright little chap this colt was.

"Saucy little blighter, too!" he added as they reached the farm, and the colt doubled back from the gate, charging Gip with his ears flattened and his head lowered.

The wise old dog wasn't beaten, though. "See how he comes in, right close behind?"

"But—Tom—he'll be kicked!"

"No, lad—that close up any flying heels would go right over t' top of 'im. A good dog learns that trick with cows."

Soon the colt was imprisoned in the yard, trotting around on the unusual hardness, sniffing inquisitively under the doors of the barn and the stables.

"Open the shed door in the corner, Nick, and we'll get 'im in there."

By moving slowly Nick hoped his limp wouldn't show. The ankle was half killing him by now, and the hardened, rutted mud didn't make it any better.

The little beast paused in terror when they edged him up to the black hole of the shed doorway. He stuck out his scraggy neck, sniffed and snorted in disgust, then tried to twist away. But Tom, Gip, and Nick were all moving in on him from behind. Turning his head he saw them, and paused. Then leaped into the gloom, his hooves rattling on the cobbles.

"We'll let him cool off, now—then move in and get a rope on him straight away so's he knows who's boss, first day—eh?" Tom smiled as he fixed the rusty door bolt. "Come and see our ol' Dinah, then, whilst we're waitin'," he went on.

Nick remembered, again, the old heavy-legged cart horse plodding up the farm lane with those piles of hay, or rattling past the end of their drive in winter with a load of logs when he and Kate had been playing in the rough bushes down by the road.

Now Dinah was dozing under the damson trees behind the farmhouse, her paintbrush tail jerking furiously from side to side in a hopeless effort to reach the evening flies as they settled on her scraggy sides.

"She's that old, is my Dinah," remarked Tom as they watched her over the gate, ". . . that old as to have no tail to speak of, see? They passed a law 'gainst choppin' 'em quite a long time since. Good thing too: take a horse's fly-whisk off him just to make him look smart, eh?" Tom nodded to himself. "Ay, our Dinah's old alreet. Won't last for never, either. It's for that I want to get yon little colt licked into shape, see? So's he can take over when Dinah's past 'n' gone. . . ." He paused, turning his long scrawny neck sideways, knowing he'd talked about dying.

Nick bit his lip. Then he spoke quite ordinarily. "But, Tom, Dinah even knows when to stop and start by herself. We'll *never* get that pony to be as good as that!"

"They never built our Lakeland walls in a day, y'know, lad. All the same," he leaned over, as if to share some great secret which Dinah and the fruit trees mustn't overhear, "I means to say we'll get on a lot faster with this colt now we've got a lad like you. I'm not as young as I were when it comes to these wild 'uns. And that ankle'll be mended up soon enough." So he'd noticed all the time. "Well, lad, do you want the job?"

Nick smiled full at him. If old Tom trusted him with this young colt—well! It hardly struck him that as the days grew shorter this little black fell pony would gobble up every spare minute. That it would mean leaving his warm bed before it was even light, that he'd have to give up . . . but that was jumping ahead anyway!

Tom must've sensed Nick was thrilled. "Well, c'mon then, and we'll do something about it straight off. Fetch some rope from the tractor shed, lad."

As Nick reached for the coils of hairy, brown rope from a nail high up on the wall he suddenly remembered: mom's washing line! Up on the felltop still! His stomach heaved over; he stood rock-still for a moment, then turned back to the shed.

The colt was pinned against the back wall when Tom opened the shed door.

"No—you stay out, Gip," Tom ordered as he moved Nick forward into the gloom with his free arm. "Light switch on the wall," he pointed. As soon as Nick had flicked it on Tom closed the door and fastened it. They were alone with the tense little horse now, with the smell of his sweaty coat and the musty cobwebs hanging from rough beams beneath the ceiling.

"Stand right up to his flank, Nick. He can't back out on account of the wall. Move fast if he kicks, though!"

Tom, meanwhile, hooked one end of the coiled rope over the forked end of his stick. Slowly, slowly, and murmuring all the time, he reached out until the prong was above the untidy mane. Then, with a twist of his wrist, he shook the rope end free so that it fell down over the pony's neck. He started nervously, but he seemed hypnotized by the soothing nonsense Tom was muttering. He stood—frozen—as the old farmer stooped forward, caught the loose end of the rope under his neck, and drew it up to form a loop. As the noose tightened the colt stepped back sharply, knocked his rump on the wall, and crouched, cornered.

Soon Tom's rough knuckles were rubbing the untidy mane. He murmured all the time until, quite soon, the hard muscles of the colt's neck seemed to relax and the frightened look went from his eye. "Now your turn, Nick!" he muttered, still in the same low voice. Nick stepped nervously across, reached out a hand, and patted the colt on the shoulder.

Immediately the pony bounded forward, his hooves clattering for a grip on the cobbles.

"What the—" Nick thought he'd been so gentle.

Tom struggled to hold the two ends of rope, and then, when all was quiet again, he explained, "You're scared as a rabbit—a horse'll always tell. Look," he went on, "it's like the stingin' nettles. Get 'em strong and firm and they won't hurt you. But fiddlin' and twitchin'—woman's stuff. This little colt'll turn out a man's horse, but it'll take something of a man to make him that way! Have another go."

This time Nick placed his hand flat on the dusty black shoulder and ran it firmly down toward the pony's ribs. The coat was rough and greasy, but the flesh was hard and knotted with muscle underneath. Already he seemed calmer.

Nick caught Tom's eye and smiled. "Right— six-thirty every mornin', eh? That way we'll have you back 'n' scrubbed and smellin' sweet as a baby in time for breakfast and school. Got to keep your mom happy you know. Now we'll leave this little lad for today, and nip into the kitchen for a cuppa tea, else my missus'll be after me. She said to be sure I brought you round to see her afore you left."

True enough, big, comfy Annie was waiting in the farm kitchen—the kettle steaming on the range and enormous slices of cherry cake laid out on a flower-patterned plate. "Made it ready for you hungry menfolk," she explained. So far as Nick was concerned they were ready for it all right!

Seven

"IT'S ALL VERY WELL, Nick," mom scolded
when he eventually arrived back for supper an
hour late, "but remember—you'll be getting
more homework from school this term. Not
every day'll be warm and long like today. Think
of the days on end when it rains nonstop up
here. If you've to be up at six you must be in bed
by eight, which'll mean missing the Wednesday
play and most of the Saturday thriller on TV."

They were at the table now. She passed him
his plate of stew—rather dried up because it
had been so long in the oven.

"I don't mind, honest I don't," Nick assured

MY FRIEND KROW

her. "This pony'll be worth giving things up for." He smiled at her across the table. To be honest, one of the best things about the colt was that it meant Nick could spend more time away from this dreary house. He knew it was wrong to think that way, but mom made him feel depressed. She didn't seem to go out except for the shopping, and when he'd come back in, her eyes were puffy and watery. He'd never known what to say when she was like that.

But now she was being firm with him. "What worries me is that old Tom Fawcett's using you as slave labor. Had it struck you that way?"

"Mom, he offered the colt to me to train—didn't force me in the least. Look—it'll be great ... really good for me, don't you see?" It was the nearest he'd ever got to admitting he needed things that were "good for him."

"There's something else, too, Nick." For a moment he thought she was going to launch in about Kate. "I haven't mentioned this to you before but . . . it's cash. Dad's been away longer than usual. And somehow the rent's got to be paid. This house is too big for us, that's what I've always said. But your dad's always had these ideas about living right in the middle of nowhere. Dear old Mr. Pulkington's offered me the job of typing out his latest book. But that won't last long, and I can't take a full-time job in Moseley because the buses are so awkward."

84

Poor mom. But what was she getting at? She leaned forward, elbows on the table, hands cupping her tea mug. "Nick," she said at last, "you wouldn't want to leave this house any more than I would, would you? Take a little bungalow in Moseley?"

He wasn't expecting that. In a rush all the happy memories of home with Kate and dad came over him, and he felt himself getting choked up. Lowering his dangerously burning eyes, he shook his head very firmly.

"But staying here will mean extra work for both of us. We can't keep old Fred on for the garden, and it's too big for me to manage by myself at the best of times. But if I'm typing Mr. Pulkington's book, I'll hardly have time for the housework and shopping. So I was relying on you for the garden . . . I mean, look at all those fallen leaves, for a start." Her eyes were gazing sadly out of the kitchen window.

Nick thought fast. No point in being vague. "OK, mom! Colt in the mornings, garden after school, and about half and half on weekends." Then, feeling heroic, he finished, "And homework after dark. Forget TV."

She smiled. "All right, then—but let's see how it goes. Don't overdo things."

Together they began to clear the table.

* * *

So things settled into this new pattern: and it

was a tight one. Every day Nick would tumble out of bed when his alarm clanged at six. On many a crisp, misty autumn morning he jogged across the fields and up the lane to Tom's; then his—yes, his!—colt would be there in the shed, shifting uneasily on his bracken bed as Nick swung open the door. Just sometimes he'd be lying down, but he always scrambled stiffly to his feet when Nick came in. He was still very nervous, but Nick didn't mind; that was half the fun, gradually winning the little fellow's trust.

The main job was to roll the heavy, wooden wheelbarrow over from the stables where Tom had left it, find an old shovel, and clean out the worst of the droppings on the shed floor.

Just once the colt scuttled past him and out into the bright, empty yard. Tom and Gip had to help Nick to inch him back in. Then Tom showed him how to wedge the wheelbarrow across the doorway while he was shoveling. "That'll keep him where he belongs, see?"

When Nick had stacked an armful of hay in the corner of the shed for his colt, he'd always give him a firm pat or two of "good-bye." At first the pony moved away from this, but later he came to put up with it. One day, perhaps, he'd actually begin to enjoy it.

Nick always stopped over at the farmhouse for a quick cup of tea with Tom and Annie before leaving. It was great to sit around that massive, wooden table, watching the old kettle come to the boil, then feel the delicious warmth of that first cup in his chilled hands.

Their clothes gave off rich farmyard smells—muck and hay and the grease off cow and pony hides.

Breakfast at home, afterwards, always seemed a letdown. Well-scrubbed, changed from friendly, smelly jeans into school trousers and newly pressed shirt, that second cup of tea was never as good as the first had been.

School continued to be misery. Nick had told Nige about the colt, but he'd never seen it, and Nick realized it would hardly sound very interesting if you weren't in some way in charge of it. As for the other kids, there was no chance of telling them about the pony. He still couldn't seem to talk with them about anything . . . just kept to himself. But it was so hurtful, feeling they were still whispering behind his back.

Mr. Pratt was certainly trying to be kind to Nick, but he did it in odd ways, seemed to treat him like a piece of dainty china that might crack. The others thought this hilarious, and it didn't take long for Nick to be branded "Pratty's pet." He knew labels like that were much easier to get than to get rid of.

If only he could have played football! But he couldn't trust his weak ankle, and he knew that if he played badly they would all be making mean remarks. What made it worse was that he'd set his heart on the school team this term. He'd missed the first selection; but he'd been watching the team in action and knew it was a good team. He was afraid that perhaps he wouldn't even get in at the mid-term trials. And Colin Stokes was captain.

The evenings were still quite light, long enough for Nick to be worn out by the time he'd slaved in the garden till it was too dark to see. Somehow that back-breaking, leaf-sweeping, rubbish-clearing, autumn-digging was the worst part of each day. He seemed so alone out there in the still, quiet garden—the garden that he and Kate had romped in, where they'd built hideouts, stalked little fluttering butterflies, where they'd laughed so much.

When all the leaves and garden rubbish were swept up, he took an old newspaper and a box of matches down the garden and lit an enormous bonfire. Then he stood, alone, and watched as the leaping flames danced higher and the thick smoke coiled away into the branches of the trees. He remembered all the other autumn bonfires: with dad, when he was home, bright and laughing; with Kate, her long black hair seeming alive in the glow; fishing out charcoal black spuds they'd buried in the embers. Bonfire night when Kate had been afraid even of the sparklers and held them at arm's length, her eyes shining with fear and excitement. No dad. No Kate. There wouldn't be a bonfire on November 5 this year. It would be no fun with just him and mom.

One of his early winter joys was to plant out the winter cabbage seedlings, the way old Fred had showed the twins the previous year. As Nick crouched now, over the rich brown furrows, he remembered how Kate's hair had fallen over her eyes as she had bent and concentrated. And she'd always been gentle with the tiny sprigs of green, patting the soil carefully round each one, talking to it as if it were alive. He planted the cabbages during the cold, dismal half-term holiday, making this job fit all the endless spare time when he could not be at the farm with Tom.

* * *

The morning Dinah died it was raining. Tom met him at the gate.

"Lost me old lass in the night, Nicky—still, she'd had a good run." For one hideous moment Nick wasn't sure whether he was talking about Annie or Dinah. Then Tom went on. "I'll leave her in the orchard till the wagon comes for her." Something drew Nick like a magnet across the muddy yard to the little orchard gate. Tom followed.

Dinah's belly rose like a great mountain

under one of the damson trees. The wet turf was churned and brown where her desperate hooves had thrashed for a footing.

"Might have been a twisted gut, might have had a heart attack, then finished herself off with strugglin' once she were down," Tom observed in a matter-of-fact voice. "No point in cuttin' her open to see. Now she's gone. Gone's gone, isn't it?"

Nick's eyes were glued to the great mound that had been Dinah. Then as he looked through the slanting rain and the mist, that hump was no longer horse . . . it seemed to be a blanket . . . heaved up by the shape of a body lying beneath it.

"Tom, can't we go in for tea . . . won't it be ready yet?"

Perhaps sensing the panic in Nick's voice, the old farmer answered calmly, "No, lad, and you've your work to do before you gets any tea. C'mon, I'll help you today. That wheelbarrow will be heavy in the mud."

It was a comfort to share the cleaning out with Tom. Good to talk about the colt, to notice the new plumpness of his sides. "He'll be a fine little horse, likely. Not as big as Dinah but just as strong. And you've got him nice and quiet, too. Should be up on his back afore long. Look, I'll show you how to clean his coat up now."

Tom reached up onto one of the beams and

brought down an ancient horsebrush, which had been lying there. He picked the cobwebs and a few of Dinah's brown hairs out of the bristles, then banged it against the wall to knock out some of the dust.

"Right, rope him up in case he turns out ticklish. Got him?"

Nick slipped a rope over the colt's neck and held the two ends under his bristly chin as Tom began to sweep the dusty black sides with long, firm strokes. Crisp shoots of bracken flew across the shed and a cloud of dust hovered in the light from the old bulb on the ceiling.

The colt seemed to love it—closed his eyes and nuzzled the back of Nick's hand with his lips.

"We'll put him out in the orchard by daytime now he's quieter, and we knows we can catch him," Tom decided somewhat breathlessly, "now Dinah's not there. And a bit o' rough weather'll bring up a nice thick winter coat on him. Wha! you little devil, you!" The colt had lashed out with a hind leg as Tom brushed a ticklish part over his ribs. "We'll larn you some manners, my lad!" And he thumped the colt good and hard on the rump with the brush. "And no softheartedness from you," he added, noticing Nick's hurt look. "Bring him up to respect you, and neither of you'll regret it."

To Nick's alarm, when they went into the

kitchen, they found Annie almost in tears.

"Not a single one left, Tom! And the beggar never eats more than two or three of them— just kills the rest out of spite!"

"That fox again? We'll have to get the foxhounds out after him. Miserable little murderer . . . all this year's chicks too, I s'pose?"

"Yes, love—every single little one of 'em. . . ."

Hearing this, Nick felt sick. Suddenly he was fighting with tears again. But it didn't seem to matter in front of Tom and Annie. "That's what Colin Stokes called me!" he mumbled. "A murderer . . . but I'm not like the fox, am I, Tom?"

Annie's arm was round his shoulders. "No, love, course you're not, and he'd no right to say you were. Look, tell us what's up. C'mon. We can't have you going home in this state, can we?"

So Nick leaned his head against her comfortable softness and slowly, painfully, the whole story came out. At last he'd finished—ending with some garbled bit about the hump of Dinah's body in the paddock and him not being like the fox.

"Aw love, here—have a cuppa tea. Now, look . . . I'll go and tell your mom that we'll be bringing you over in the van when Tom goes in to the market. I should plan on a quiet day at home, lad. Forget school for today. You've been overdoin' it lately by the looks of it."

When she went out to phone, Tom coughed and leaned towards him over the table. Nick suddenly felt stupid and babyish. After all, it was Tom who'd told him it would take a man to make the colt a man's horse, wasn't it?

"Look, lad, you mustn't take it badly like this. They always says, 'The good Lord gives and the good Lord takes away.' He knows what he's doin' alreet. Dinah's gone old; your Kate went young. But believe me—he knows best, and he took 'em both when he wanted 'em."

Nick looked at the old farmer's work-lined hands wrapped around the tea mug. Then he raised his eyes to the brown, scraggy face, the greasy cap shoved back to show a white, un-tanned forehead.

"Believe me," Tom went on, "with three thousand sheep on your hands like I have, you learns to live with death. And often enough a young ewe'll die just afore she brings a couple of bonny lambs into the world and I loses the lot. Or they breaks through a fence I've not mended well and drowns in the brook, because their fleeces is too heavy for them to swim across. . . . I tells you, Nick-me-lad, if I blamed meself every time, I'd have given up farmin' years back. But I sez, 'Well, the good Lord knows I'm a farmer, and he knows I'm not a perfect farmer, but he's on my side all the same.

Elsewise I'd have given up long ago.'" Tom stopped. He pushed his cap a bit farther back so that he could scratch an itchy spot on his head.

Annie returned from the phone. "Your mom says 'no hurry'—and p'rhaps you'd better have your breakfast with us for today. You'll take porridge and boiled eggs? It's the last we'll have for a while," she laughed bravely, "till I gets some more hens."

Nick grinned at her. "Yes—I'll eat the lot, thanks." He felt much better already. Tom was talking sense. Discovering that Tom trusted the same Lord Jesus whom Kate had gone to made Nick feel different about things, less lonely and empty. Maybe Uncle Rog had been right, and maybe Jesus was not such a faraway, storybook person either.

But now Tom was changing the subject completely. He leaned back and lit up his pipe, looking at Nick man-to-man. "Well, what you going to call yon colt, eh? It's time he knew who he was!"

Funnily, Nick hadn't given a thought to this yet. But he felt honored that here was Tom, asking *him* to choose . . .

"I'll think about it, Tom . . . I'll let you know."

Eight

"SIT AT THE TABLE, Nick. I'll brew up some tea; then we can have a good talk."

Back in the kitchen at home, Nick couldn't believe his ears. His mom wanted to talk . . . perhaps Annie had said something on the phone?

But he was feeling so confused, anyway, that—yes—perhaps it'd be best to have a good talk—get it over with.

"So sad about old Dinah," mom began as she poured the tea, which Nick didn't really want. "But animals can't last forever, can they, love?" Then, seeing Nick was staring into his mug and didn't know what to say, she pressed on, "Still, funny how it should've started you off. After all, you've got that pony, haven't you?"

Why did she have to turn everything into stupid questions like that? Nick wondered. "S'pose so," he muttered, just for something to say. He looked up. Her face was red, perhaps from standing over the kettle. But it struck him then that she was going through the same kind of misery that he was. The wretchedness was tightening in on them both again. Nick had to last out against it.

"Mom—it wasn't just Dinah. It was . . . the lump of her, just like . . . just like Kate under the blanket," he blurted, "and the fox and the chickens was—like Colin said I was, a murderer!"

Mom was silent for several long seconds. Nick's words seemed to echo round the walls of the big kitchen. She took him up on the one thing she'd really been able to understand from what he'd said.

"Colin Stokes said you were a murderer? Oh, Nicky!" Mom's arms were around him, and she was holding him very tightly, and crying.

Nick was so surprised that he just sat there, stiff, and not knowing what to do.

At last she took one hand away to find a hanky in her apron pocket. Then, giving her nose a good blow, she moved back to her chair and began to talk awkwardly. "Don't you take any notice of that Colin Stokes! I'd have Mr. Pratt on to him if I thought it'd do any good, but I know the kids would just take it out on you afterwards."

She paused for a moment, then plowed on. "Nick, I want to tell you something . . . very honest. It's just that, I've been really hating you over these last weeks about Kate."

Nick sat up and stared. She was sobbing quietly still, and didn't want to look straight at him. Then words started drifting into his mind. Uncle Rog's words as they'd driven back round the lake, "You've got to make her want to forgive you . . . to ask God's help to forgive you. And it won't be easy because she's not a lady who talks to God easily." He gulped, realizing how right Uncle Rog had been. Surely only God could get them out of this mess. Otherwise, wouldn't she just hate him forever?

His mind was racing now, in search of words to say. But mom beat him to it. "Nicky," she said softly, leaning forward, her elbows on the table, hands cupping her chin. "Nicky, this is going to sound silly to you—it's just something Aunt Meg was always saying when she was here. She knew how I was feeling about you and she just said—over and over—'Look what Jesus did for us when he died, love. When we ask him, he forgives us for *everything*. So can't you trust

Jesus and begin to forgive Nicky?' " Mom paused. "Oh, I'm sorry, love. It's probably all dutch to you, but, somehow, it's working for me. Already I don't feel so bad about you."

Her reddened eyes met Nick's in a frightened kind of way. They looked straight at each other—and understood for the first time since the accident.

Nick felt very close to her—at last. And he felt, somehow, grown-up. He wanted to hug and hold her—to do something for her, anything.

They sat for a little longer, peacefully, gazing at the cold teapot and the cold toast on the chipped daisy-patterned plate. Then "Come on, can't sit here all day!" and Nick helped her with the washing up.

Later, he went up quietly to Kate's room and stood for a while by her window, watching the steady rain beating down on his cabbage seedlings outside. It was then he decided that he'd call the colt Crow. After Kate. And because he was black, like her hair. What's more—yes—it'd be Krow-with-a-*K*. He could have Kate's *K*, too. And just as Nick had so often failed to be sensible and gentle with Kate, he'd make up for it by the way he treated Krow. At least, he'd try, and that was a start.

*   *   *

It was an odd day. Nick felt worn out and yet

unreasonably happy. Over lunch he talked and talked to mom: about the mid-term football trials next week and his chances for the team, and about the beautiful little horse that—stupidly—he had dreamed Krow might become. He chatted on as he hadn't done all these weeks. "You must make her want to forgive you." Yes, he must try.

The afternoon seemed very long. It was still pouring. Nick stood by the sitting-room window, staring out through the clear, smeared drops on the glass. It had been that sort of day . . . a great wash-clean day. He felt fresh and clean, too.

Mom was on the sofa behind him mending what she called his "colt clothes." "Good thing you got the digging done and the cabbage seedlings planted before all this rain," she remarked.

"Yes, but I want something new to do now, mom." He turned to her. "Something indoors because it's dark so soon in the evenings." Then he added, "All the things I like doing need Kate or dad to join in." It was such a relief to be able to say that.

Mom didn't snap at him for it. There was a long, friendly silence as she stitched on. Nick watched her.

"I'd like to do something for Christmas, a present for someone," he said at last.

"Tell you what . . ." she dropped the crumpled jeans into her lap. "How about making a manger for the colt for Christmas?"

"Yes! And that'd be a sort of present for Tom, too!" he added excitedly, "because it would keep the hay from getting trampled on the bracken and wasted." Then his heart sank. "But what'll I make it out of? I'd need so many tools—a plane, chisel, hammer, screws, screwdriver, saw—and a vice and a bench . . ." Before he'd finished he was reddening because he had realized what this meant. So had she.

"I know dad won't mind if you use his things, Nick. You're not a baby anymore. The workbench is all cluttered up with my bowls of spring bulbs, but they can come out into the house now."

"I think I can manage," Nick went on, slightly doubtful. "Dad taught me quite a lot."

"That's up to you," mom remarked. "But you'll have to start by making a list of the wood lengths you'll need. Challoners' in Moseley should have them."

"We'll have to go in on a Saturday, though." Nick was wondering if it would come out of yard-time or Krow-time.

"We'll go in the morning; the yard's tidy enough by now," mom said. "You sound as if you need every moment you've got for that pony."

"Oh, and mom, I'm going to call him 'Krow,' because . . . because . . ." At the last minute, Nick couldn't manage to tell her the rather complicated reason for calling the pony Crow, let alone Krow-with-a-*K*, so he just said, "because he's all black and a bit scraggy, still."

"Well, I just hope he's got better table manners than most crows. After all, he's going to be eating out of a handmade manger."

Nine

THAT EVENING THE RAIN cleared and the
weather turned much colder. In the night it
snowed, a very early fall, but thick and soft.
When Nick woke on Saturday morning, he
thought it must be very early still, it seemed so
dark through the window. He rolled over and
relaxed into the soft mattress again, looking
forward to an hour of dozing before he'd have
to get up. This was marvelous . . . it would be
the same every weekend since they'd decided
last night that he should do his colt in the afternoons on Saturday and Sunday, so he could
sleep in.

"Nick! Come on, sleepyhead! The Moseley bus goes in twenty minutes! Your egg's done... aren't you even dressed yet?"

Leaping to his feet and staggering to the window, he groaned. The linoleum was freezing beneath his feet. A thick, gray blanket of cloud hung low on the fells, and the valley floor was white. Not a spot of color in sight, but like a black-and-white film when you are used to color.

They had a long, cold wait at the bottom of the drive, and when the bus eventually growled cautiously round the bend in very low gear, it was already twelve minutes late. Ken's welcoming smile warmed them as they stepped on board. Then the excitement began! Before they'd reached Moseley, they'd passed three abandoned cars, and a van skewed into a wall with its hood buckled in the air. And whenever the bus passed under a low tree, it knocked off a great wet splattering of snow that banged down onto its tin roof.

They found a book in the library called, "A Guide to Elementary Carpentry Techniques." Nick thought it sounded a bit heavy, but there were some good pictures inside.

He was excited about the wood itself though it was sad going to Challoners, because he and dad often used to sneak off there during boring shopping expeditions when mom and Kate seemed to spend centuries in the supermarket. Now mom had no Kate to go off with. Being Saturday, the boss—Jack Challoner—wasn't around. There was just a thick-looking lad with long, greasy hair. Trying to sound at least fourteen, Nick read out his cutting list.

"Yer—reckons as what we can find something what'll do. Usually keep some scraps out the back for little jobs like that." And the youth slunk off towards the yard behind the workshop.

"Just a minute, lad," called mom, who couldn't bear rude, hairy young men, anyway. He turned on his heel and looked back.

"I'm not putting up with any old scraps. We want decent wood and we'll pay a decent price. Mr. Challoner knows us," she added for good measure, "and he's always dealt very fairly with us."

"Look, don't let it worry you, missus," the lad explained as though he were facing a couple of dumb six-year-olds. "When I says 'scrap' I means 'off-cuts.' Seeing as what you only wants fairly short bits, it's not worth cuttin' up long planks when we've got bits left over from bigger jobs—just the same quality wood."

Yes, yes, all right—they understood. But he wouldn't let them off without a forced, sneering smile.

Several times he wandered through from the

back with just one or two pieces of wood. Once he stopped to light up a cigarette then stood for half a minute drawing deeply on it before shuffling off towards the yard again.

Mom looked despairingly at Nick. "We *are* in somewhat of a hurry," she shouted after him, hiding her impatience reasonably well.

The boy paused, turned back. "Look, ma'am," he came closer and puffed smoke into their faces, "I wants you to have the best—the very best. And that takes time, that does." And off he went again. This time, mom and Nick smiled at each other.

At last the pile of wood was tied up on the bench, a bill added up on the back of the cigarette packet, and mom wrote out a check.

"Mmmm—Braithwaite? So you'll be Nick, then, what goes to my brother's school?"

"Brother?" Nick asked politely. "Oh—what's his name then?"

"Well, same as mine, not surprising: Stokes—Colin Stokes."

And with that he took mom's check and disappeared.

Mom was a bit disgusted about the whole business. Nick was stunned by those last words, which the hairy boy had puffed at them through the haze of smoke.

"Never mind," Nick assured mom after they'd complained most of the way home on the bus. "My ankle's good as new now, so I'll be in the next trials for the junior team. Then I'll show him." He had to say that just to make her feel she had someone to protect her and win revenge against that rude shop boy.

Yes, they'd be holding the trials as soon as this snow cleared. Nick just wished he was as sure as he'd sounded about winning a place on the team. Jogging over to the farm every morning must be helping to get him fit, but he hadn't touched a ball for months. After all those hours kicking a ball about on the concrete drive with Kate, he couldn't face banging the ball up against their coal-house door by himself.

* * *

"Colt's in the orchard," Tom yelled from the cow stable as he saw Nick trotting up through the slush into the farmyard.

"Krow, you mean!"

"Crow is it, then? Well, at least you're not expectin' him to turn into a luvly white swan. And you're probably right there! See if you can fetch him in yourself, lad. I'm just finishin' off the milkin'."

Nick found the rough rope halter on the usual hook behind the shed door. Then, gathering up a fistful of hay from the barn floor on the way past, he went to the orchard gate. The snow was wet and greasy, but in a strange way the orchard looked beautiful:

black branches and twigs of the damson trees spread out in a pattern of thick and fine lines against the dull whiteness of the snow. Then there were the strong, dark trunks of the trees and, in the distance, the spiked threads of a rickety barbed-wire fence, which cut the orchard off from the fell beyond.

"Krow! Krow! Krow!" Nick caught sight of the pony as he stepped forward from the shelter of the barn wall on hearing his voice. His coat was already thick and warm, and it bristled like a rabbit's in the cold, wintry air. A splattering of snow must've just fallen onto him from the barn gutter. It was melting down his rump like a smeared patch.

Nick had never caught him alone before, but Tom had once said, "They'll come to the hand that feeds 'em." On that reckoning, Krow should come to him easily enough. After all, think of all the hay Nick had lugged into his shed during these weeks.

Nick walked carefully towards the pony across the slushy snow—talking, even nonsense—to calm him, just as Tom did.

Poor Krow was fed up after hours scraping at the miserable white stuff that had smothered his short, sweet grass. He snorted crossly through his nostrils. It was so cold that he seemed to blow out a great cloud of smoke. Then, tossing his head briskly, he set off across the orchard at a fast trot, lowering his neck now and then to duck under the sweeping branches of the fruit trees. Nick moved towards him, then—remembering—nipped back to fasten the wicket gate he'd left open.

When Krow reached the fence he turned, paused, and then pranced away again, his hooves churning up clods of wet snow that smacked down behind him and excited him to move faster, faster. Soon he was pounding round in a big circle, knocking snow from the trees, slithering every time he had to turn, his breath sweeping back past his sides in streaky clouds.

Nick couldn't hope to keep up but stood near the middle of his circle, talking to the pony still. But his voice soon became high and excited. Finally he couldn't resist it . . . he let loose the end of the halter rope and flicked it across the black rump as it passed . . . just lightly, just enough to tip the pony into a splendid, pounding gallop.

He bucked furiously when he felt the rope: head down, heels up. For a few strides he couldn't see where he was going. Then there was a ripping and thrashing of wire, and a stamping of hooves in panic as the coils of wire from the fence tightened around his legs and the spikes cut through his woolly fur. Finally he was terribly still.

Tom arrived at the orchard gate just at that moment. "Hold it!" he shouted. "Still as a rock, Nicky. I'll get the cutters." In a moment he was back. He strode across the orchard and moved in close to the trembling, steaming colt. "Rope—halter, Nick, quick." Within seconds Tom had taken the rope and slipped a noose around Krow's face. "Filthy, filthy stuff, barbed wire—and rusty, at that. Wish I could afford to do without it," he muttered as he summed up the damage. "I'll have to hold him, lad—else if he dives or jumps about you wouldn't be able to keep him steady and he'd do himself even more damage. So you'll have to take these."

Nick took the cutters, knelt in the snow, and, obeying Tom's slow, careful instructions, set about slicing through the tangle of wire around Krow's legs. Luckily his fur covered the worst of the cuts, but some of it was already smoothed into points from which blood dripped steadily onto the white snow . . . like the bright, beaded blood that had dripped from Kate's hand as she'd stood, white-faced and terrified, on that scree. No, he mustn't think about it.

"Get him away off the fence," was Tom's next order. "We can cut the bits of wire out of his leg hair later." All the same, it took about ten minutes to cut all the strands so that each leg was free from the fence.

"His tail, Tom! That's all caught up, too."

"Chop if off, lad. Let's get him away from the fence, quick as we can."

Nick was horrified! Cut Krow's beautiful tail short and stumpy like Dinah's! No, it should be long and wavy, soft and well-brushed. He seemed to hear Kate's voice taunting him, now, "Mom told me I *deserved* lovely hair 'cause I brush it every night."

"No, Tom." Nick's voice was angry. "No, I'll free it like the legs, snipping with the cutters."

Before Tom had time to argue, Nick was behind Krow's rump, leaning to grip the coils of wire with the cutters.

Just as Nick had snipped and tugged the hair free, the colt shifted his hooves a little. Perhaps he realized he was almost out of the cruel barbs. He backed, suddenly. The cutters jabbed sharply into his rump and, in a flash, he'd lashed out at Nick with a hind leg. Nick fell into the snow, clasping his knee and howling.

"Shut up, lad, and get onto your feet! Lie there and he'll get at you again!" Tom barked, struggling to hold Krow forward.

But Nick's howls weren't baby's howls. Within minutes the knee was coming up like a balloon. He managed to hobble to the kitchen and find Annie, who bandaged it with a cold-water pad, while Tom led the colt slowly around to the shed.

110

So, for the second time in two days, Nick was ferried home in the old farm van.

* * *

"And our P.E. teacher said we'd have the team trials next week," Nick wailed to his mom. "Now what chance have I got?"

"Nicky!" she calmed him. "Bawling'll get you nowhere. Look, if I take the kitchen stool and the paraffin heater out to the workshop, you could start planing wood for the manger."

"Blinkin' manger! Think that old black nag's getting a manger from me?"

"Nicky! Don't talk like that. And that wood cost me money. And you know he only kicked out because he was hurt and frightened. He didn't mean to hit you."

Nick suddenly remembered why it had all happened. The rope end, the bucking, the clouds of hot breath.

"In any case," mom continued, *"you've* got to learn to forgive, too!"

Nick didn't wait to hear more. He was hobbling out through the back door towards the workshop. Yes, that manger would be finished by Christmas all right.

Later that evening mom let Nick call Tom. Yes, Krow was all right. But the vet had come to give him an injection because the wire had been so rusty. The cuts should heal eventually and Krow still had his long, glossy tail!

Ten

THAT KIND OF EARLY SNOW never lasts long. By Monday there were wet blotches, still, high on the fells. But the valley was a soggy green again. The cloud had heaved itself back into the sky-proper, and a brisk wind was drying out the wet earth.

"Such a shame, 'bout that leg," teased a rough voice as Nick stood shivering in the school yard on the way back from a boring gym lesson. Boring for Nick, at least, who could only do the arm exercises. He paused, looked around. Colin Stokes was standing there. "Would've thought you'd a chance for the team if you hadn't done it in. What a shame, then, eh?"

Nick couldn't think what to say.

"Never mind—might make goalie next term," Colin carried on. He knew very well that Nick would play center or nothing. An attacking player wouldn't be seen dead between the posts.

"Goalie, my foot!" Nick exploded. "Just you wait. I'll *murder* you at center once this leg's better."

"Murder me, too, eh?" A sly smile spread across Colin's face.

For a moment the two boys stood facing each other. Then Mr. Pratt's lanky form appeared in the doorway, and he was calling, "It'll be lunch-time before some of you reach my lesson. Come on!"

Both boys hurried into the cloakroom to hang up their parkas.

"And I hear mummy took us to buy some itsy bitsy wood on Saturday to make a cradle, eh?" Colin whispered in a takeoff of a toddler's voice, just as they reached the classroom door.

Nick hadn't time to answer. Colin had timed his remark just right! They found their places and slumped into them while the other kids turned to watch.

"Right!" announced Mr. Pratt. "Now, having got you all here, I think it's about time I went off duty, eh? It's taken you long enough." A polite titter rose from the class, mainly from the girls.

"Since," he continued, "certain of the boys seem better than the school staff at planning the timetable," he paused a moment, fixing Nick and Colin with his eye, "perhaps they'd care to take over the lesson as well. During the past four weeks I've been telling you about men who've given their lives for what they believe in. Now it's your turn to do something—all I'm going to say is that the theme is 'Martyrdom and Self-sacrifice' . . ."

One or two of the girls tittered again. "What's that when it's at home?" someone whispered.

"Nicholas Braithwaite!" Mr. Pratt called. Nick groaned to himself. Now what? "Nicholas. You will lead one group please. You will explore 'Martyrdom and Self-sacrifice' through the medium of drama. I'll give you a story, and it's up to you what you do with it. You can work on this with—er, let's see . . . Colin Stokes, Tony Bell, Nancy Hodgson, Karen Nicholson, and Peter Barker. Here's the story. I suggest you settle in the far corner. I'll be over soon to see how you're getting on."

They all liked drama. But Nick was stunned. What a rotten subject. "Martyrdom and Self-sacrifice," not to mention a lousy group like this and, worst of all, Colin Stokes.

114

Mr. Pratt handed him an ancient, musty book. A piece of paper was sticking out halfway through. "That's the page," he told him. "I think you'll find that particular story is appropriate . . . particularly to a dramatic presentation."

"Why can't he just say, 'Do a play'?" whispered Tony as they all moved over to the far corner with their chairs.

"My mom goes to dramatics on Monday, and sometimes when she comes back she's still got greasepaint in her hair. . . ." That was Nancy.

Colin had sat himself down in the best position, so he could dangle his arms over the radiator.

Rather than catch his eye, Nick fumbled straight through to the marked page. "Gaw Hong and the Headhunters" it was called.

"Listen to this!" he announced. "Gaw Hong and the Headhunters." Nancy and Karen were hugging themselves with controlled giggling. "Right—shut up, you two . . . oh, Colin," he looked the bigger boy right in the eye, "could you read the story through so we all know what's going on?"

That silenced them. All eyes were fixed on the two boys, watching, waiting. Amazed.

Still slumped against the radiator, Colin reached out a hand and took the book roughly from Nick. "Don't see why not." After all, as

Nick had realized, he was either going to have to read it himself or sit there and listen while someone else, perhaps even Nick, read it at him.

"Everyone sittin' comfortable? Here goes." He wasn't a very fast reader, but he did have a way with him—a strong voice, almost threatening, "Listen, or else!" You had to listen. No fidgeting, not even from the girls.

" '. . . Gaw Hong was guvn'r of an island in the South Pacific Ocean.' " Karen and Nancy were giggling softly again. " '. . . and the natives there were feared for miles around on account of their traditions of head-hunting. In fact, they were so violent that Gaw Hong was the third guvn'r to the island in two years. The others had all been eaten up by the wild islanders!' " Colin looked up, his eyes shining.

" 'Gaw Hong, however, was a good, brave man.' " (Gentle "Aaah!" from Nancy.) " 'He was not afraid of spears and stories of bloody murders.' " ("Whoops, watch it!" from Nancy. "Shut up, Nancy, or you're out of this," Nick snapped, then nodded to Colin to carry on.)

" 'One day he went into the jungle with only his manservant and marched bravely right into the village of the native chief himself. His warriors were poundin' round the fire in a big circle. Over the fire hung a steamin' pot, quite large enough to take a man.

" ' "Peace be with you," he called in a brave voice, "for I come in the name o' peace." The warriors ceased from their wild dance and stared at this noble man.

" ' "Why can't we live in harmony together, brother?" asked Gaw Hong as he approached the chief's skull-decorated throne.

" ' "It is our god, Tamba," the chief replied in a great, deep voice. "We must have a sacrifice once every moon, a human sacrifice. Otherwise Tamba'll send terrible diseases among our cattle, and when they are all dead, then we shall die, too, for we shall have nothing to eat. Listen, I've a sick cow even now . . ." He paused and Gaw Hong heard, sure enough, the sad mooing of a dying cow behind one of the village huts.' "

At this point Tony broke in with his own bellowing version of a dying cow. Nick noticed Mr. Pratt's head rise from the books he was marking. He looked over in their direction.

"Aw, shut up, Tony. You're pathetic. Let's go on, Colin. We'll kick Tony out if he does it again." Colin seemed glad Nick had once more cleared the way for him to carry on reading. "Right . . . where was I? Ah, here. . . .

" ' "Nonsense," replied Gaw Hong. "All you need is medicines for your cows. I'll have them sent out tomorrow." At this the chief grew angry. "So you cheat Tamba?"

" 'For a moment there was silence. Then Gaw

Hong replied, quietly, "Let us strike a bargain, chief. We will give Tamba just one more sacrifice. If that does not work, you will be sent medicines. If those are successful, you swear to me there'll be no more bloodshed?"

" 'The chief thought a while, then drew his finger sharply across his throat.' " (Blood-curdling gurgle from Karen. Colin stopped. Nick glared at her. She went red. Colin carried on reading.) " ' "I swear I will keep this bargain, Gaw Hong. Send one man—alone—into the forest at dawn tomorrow. After that I will accept your medicines for my cows, and no stranger will suffer at the hands of my warriors."

" 'Accordingly, at dawn a warrior was stationed in a tall tree beside the track through the jungle. As the sun's first rays came through the thick leaves, he spied a tall figure approachin' along the path. In a moment he had fixed an arrow to his bow, taken aim, and shot. The man fell instantly, the arrow pierced through his heart.

" 'Warriors were already dancin' round the fire when he turned up at the village. The chief was throned in his most splendid robes. The sweat-streaked headhunter dashed to the foot of the throne.

" ' "One dead masser! One dead!" And he held the head up by the hair. Instantly there was a terrible hush. For the head was none other than that of Gaw Hong himself.' "

Colin closed the book with a slap, slumped back against the radiator, and announced smugly, "That's it, fans." They were all pretty stunned. Even the girls were sitting stock-still with their mouths half open.

Nick felt as if the story had knocked the breath right out of him, but he hadn't time now to wonder exactly why.

"It's obvious the girls'll have to be the warriors," he declared.

"What!" they exploded.

"Well," he explained, "It'll give you a chance to show off your dancing. And I can show you, too, because my Uncle Roger's been to Africa and he showed me. Then Tony can be the warrior who shoots Gaw Hong. That leaves just Gaw Hong and the chief . . . oh, and Gaw Hong's servant."

"Can I be that?" Peter broke in, clearly terrified of being given a big part.

Nick looked across at Colin. That meant they were left with the two main parts: the headhunter and the man who gets murdered.

"You'll be the guvn'r, Nick. I'll be the chief." Colin was smiling.

They started to practice the play. The girls got giggly and silly again, and it took both Colin and Nick to keep them in order. The other two boys were all right, but a bit feeble.

"Not bad, not bad at all—in fact it's shaping up quite nicely," commented Mr. Pratt as he wandered over halfway through and caught them doing the sick-cow bit. "See if you can be fit to act for the rest of the class by twelve-fifteen."

That gave them only twenty minutes. Not nearly long enough! At least it made the girls pull themselves together and really try, though Peter and Tony looked even more terrified now.

When they came to the real thing, Nick found he was sweating. So was Colin, though he didn't have to rush around as much as Nick did. But they'd both really flung themselves into their parts, and the girls were doing some fantastic dancing. They got so carried away that they didn't seem to hear the sly remarks of Tracey Milner and Tim Askham who were sitting in the front row of their audience.

For the last scene, Nick stood aside while Tony rushed on with the wastepaper basket (it was supposed to contain Nick's head). He tipped it up at Colin's feet and there was a fabulous silence. "Gaw Hong!" Colin yelled at last. "Oh, my friend! And because you have done this I *swear* there will be no more head-hunting!"

Then everyone was clapping. Mr. Pratt

shouted, "Well done, all of you! Splendid stuff!"

Which was great. Nick felt good, even though his knee was killing him. He knew Colin was pleased, too. But he wasn't sure what would happen when the bell rang. When it did, he made himself wait back a little so that he went out into the yard with Colin.

"Better than math, I s'pose," Colin remarked.

"Mmm," Nick agreed. "Shame we don't do it every week like that." He looked sideways at Colin for a moment. The big boy was thoughtful.

"I don't get what it's got to do with religious ed."

Nick took a deep breath. "I reckoned it was about—like—as if it was about Kate!"

Colin looked at him sharply, as he sat down on the low wall at the end of the playground. "You *what?*"

"Well, because Gaw Hong gave his life up, all the warriors could carry on living, but in a better sort of way. And that's how Kate's dying seems . . . to me. I'm getting to be different now."

They were both sitting side by side on the wall now. Several of the other kids were watching them curiously, but they hardly noticed.

Nick felt he must plow on with what he was

saying, "Col, see, it's a bit like Jesus dying as well—when he'd done nothing wrong. But he even *wanted* to do it so we'd turn out better. And now things are *much* better between mom and me."

Colin looked slightly dazed after all that. "It's all right for you," he said at last. "You've got a decent mom anyway. My family is all a bloomin' dead loss!" He was looking down, angrily, picking a scab on the top of his knee.

"But you can't say that about your family!" Nick was shocked. "At least you've got a dad around, who's not away at sea all the time, and you've got that brother. But my sister's *dead!*"

"You've no idea," Colin continued. "Dad's always out with his truck, away for the best part of a week, usually. And when he's back mom's screamin' her head off at him all the time. When he's away, she drinks herself stupid every night. Then our Geoff—the one you met at Challoners'—he's always getting yelled at for bringing some girl home what looks awful, and they plays his records much too loud—see we only has a little house, and the walls is thin as paper."

Now that he'd got going, Nick thought he'd never stop.

"Weekends is worst of all. Mom goes out to clean at a hotel—that gives us a bit of peace at home, but then its gets lonely. I has to fix me own grub and that. Then by six Geoff's back from Challoners' with his Tina, and they usually kicks me out so's they can have the place to themselves. That's why, see, I wants to stay captain of the football. It gives me something to do on Saturdays."

All this hit Nick like a rockfall. He didn't even know what to say. But the bell had gone for first lunch (he was on second that week). Colin eased himself off the wall and set off for the dining hall. Nick just had time to say, "I see it, now. I get what you mean."

As soon as Colin had disappeared, Nige—who had been watching all this from a distance—came bounding over. "What on earth was all that about?"

Nick laughed, and laughed more when he realized what had started it all.

"Well," he told Nige, "funny thing is, it was all to do with that mumbo-jumbo dancing your dad showed us up in the attic last winter!"

Eleven

"HAD A GOOD DAY then?" Mom was busy stirring some soup for tea when Nick burst into the kitchen that evening.

"Fantastic, mom!" She glanced up for a moment. It was months since she had heard him sounding so cheerful. Then he launched into a rambling version of the Gaw Hong story, the way Mr. Pratt had been so pleased about their play, and the time he'd spent with Colin out on the wall. By the time they had set the table and were both crouched over bowls of hot soup, he'd just about told her everything.

"What I wondered," he ended triumphantly,

"was whether some weekends maybe we could have Colin out here with us? And he can help with Krow. There's . . . even Kate's room for him so he can stay overnight."

He stopped there. Maybe he'd gone too far. Mom's eyes—kind now—were on him, and she smiled. "Fine, fine, Nicky. That's a great idea." But her face was still sad.

"Mom, what's happened? What's the matter?"

She put her spoon down on the plate. "It's just that exactly a year ago today your dad went away to sea. It was a cold, gray day just like this one. Oh, how I do miss him!" She paused, then her face brightened. "But with you coming bouncing in like that, I feel better already. Nick, I'm going to sit down and write to him tonight, a really happy letter telling him I don't mind if he has to be away so much. That I can take it if it's the way God wants things to be for the moment. I've wanted to be able to write to him like that for so long now. But my letters always turn out grumpy and it's no wonder he doesn't write back."

Her face was lovely and peaceful now. Nick wanted to be able to tell Colin about this. After all, it was partly because they'd made up wasn't it?

Mom wanted to say something else. "But there is still the money problem, Nick. At this rate I'll have finished Mr. Pulkington's book by Christmas. Then that's it. And I did want to give Meg and Roger a good present because they've been so good to us."

"But where does the money go, mom? We're hardly big spenders."

"Mostly on the rent for this place. I've always worried so much about the rent. And that's made me angry with your dad when he comes home almost broke, because he's spent most of his pay on having a good time with the navy, or buying presents for you two. But now . . . I don't feel so bitter about that. I'm just finding I can trust God now. It's so marvelous not worrying all the time."

"That's like Tom," Nick told her. "He said he'd have left farming years ago if he hadn't known God was on his side, no matter what."

"Right, Nick. So that means we have Colin out here as often as you want, and somehow, we'll find a way of feeding him! And we'll face the springtime when it comes."

Nick laughed with her, and didn't feel quite so bad about taking the extra slice of cake he'd had his eye on.

* * *

"I got really stuck with this manger I'm making yesterday evening," he told Colin at break the next day. "I really needed another hand. But mom was busy writing to dad, so I didn't want to disturb her. She said it was easier to write because we'd made up!"

Colin smiled. They were in the yard. He was dribbling a tiny stone with the tip of his gym shoes. "But what's all that about a manger. You doing some training for the team still?" He laughed. "You'll never get center forward off me in a lifetime!"

Nick laughed, too. After all, he knew why the team meant so much to Colin, now.

"Well, what's this manger then?"

"Oh, that's for Krow."

"Crow? You what?"

"Oh—you know that wood we bought off your brother in Challoners'? Well, it wasn't to make a cradle. It was for a manger for Christmas so's Krow needn't eat his hay off the bracken."

"Yes—but *who is Crow?*"

Nick realized that—all these weeks—he'd never told anyone but Nigel about his pony. "Just shows how well I scrub myself before I come down to school!" he laughed. "None of you've even smelled him!" Then he began telling Colin all about his little, black colt with the coarse, woolly coat and the long tail. And even the way they'd saved that tail from being cut short. Which explained Nick's limp, too.

"Sounds all right," Colin commented. "I never bin close to a horse—only on TV."

127

"Thing is, he'll be strong enough to ride, soon, and Tom says it takes two and he hasn't got the time. You need someone to hold him while the other person gets on . . . things like that."

Colin looked at him straight. "I could do that for you, if you'd let me. It'd be better'n watching the racin' on TV with me dad at the weekends, with him swearin' every time he's backed a loser!"

Twelve

NICK HOPED TOM and Annie had forgotten everything he'd said to them about Colin. It seemed they had. Tom was delighted when the two boys turned up together that Saturday. "With two pairs o' hands we'll soon get young Nick up on him!" He took a quick liking to Colin. After all, the boy was solid, tough and sensible enough with the pony, seeing he'd never been near one before.

First Tom finished his milking. So Nick took Col over to the orchard, and quietly they caught Krow and took him over to the shed. Then Nick brushed him while Col held the halter and made friends with the pony. Nick worked gently over the wire-cut scabs, telling Col just how the coils had snaked around Krow's legs.

"Funny, thought he'd be bigger. Must've got the wrong idea from them racehorses on TV!"

"But fell ponies are always small!" Nick coughed; it was getting dusty. "But they're dead tough. Bet you Krow could carry Tom, though his legs'd touch the ground on each side!" They laughed.

"Beg yer pardons?" Tom's lanky figure filled the shed doorway. "That fur's coming up nice and shiny, now. It'd make my Annie a nice fur coat 'gainst these cold winds." Before Nick had time to explode, Tom had taken the halter rope from Colin and told him to stand by Krow's shoulder.

"Right, Nick, put that brush up on the beam. You're getting as vain about your pony as an old woman. Now . . . lean your top half over his back, rest your weight on him, and kick your feet off the floor if you feels safe enough."

Nick's chest was buried in Krow's glossy coat. He did get his feet off the bracken after a while. Then his whole weight was resting on Krow's back. The other two were very quiet. Krow moved a little and Nick felt his backbone stiffen.

"Right, Colin me lad, take Nick's left foot and

boost him gently over. Nick, keep your top half lying low. If he looks back and sees you stickin' up high off his back, then he will start to dance, no mistake!"

So, gently, Colin took Nick's ankle—the one he'd twisted. Very gently, he pushed it up. Nick kept the knee stiff. Slowly, his body rose till he could slip the other leg over Krow's back. There he crouched, his heart thudding against Krow's neck . . . but he was there!

"That was fantastic!" he gasped as he slithered to the floor a few minutes later.

"Mr. Fawcett, can I have a go now, eh?" Colin asked.

"Trouble is, lad, you're that much heavier. Give him a few weeks, say, till Christmas, so he can build up some weight-liftin' muscles, then we'll see."

It was fair, really. Col had his football on Saturday mornings, then he came out on the bus and helped Nick in the afternoons. For hours he just led him around the farm on his beautiful, hairy Krow. To start with they stayed in the orchard, just in case the pony got loose. But later the three of them, usually with Gip in tow, as well, wandered off down the lane and into the valley meadows.

"It's right grand," Tom declared one frosty Sunday, "that you've got Colin to help. I couldn't have spared the time with all me ditchin' and 'edgin' at this time o' year."

"But won't Krow be able to go without being led, one day?" Nick asked.

"Well, Nick me lad," Tom looked serious, "trouble is, I haven't the tackle for riding horses. I've only got cart horse gear, see? Tell you what, though. With the two o' you it'll take only half the time to save up for a proper little bridle, eh? You won't be wantin' a saddle, girl's stuff, that." All three of them laughed.

So began the great save. It meant that both the boys dug out their dads' old bikes and patched them up. Nick was tall enough, with the seat lowered, to be just safe. Mom said, yes, he could ride it to school each day—and that saved ten pence a day in bus fares. Col saved twenty-two pence a day as he had further to come, but his mom wouldn't let him bike when the weather was bad—said she couldn't cope with his wet clothes. So, counting the wet days, their savings worked out about the same. Nige, of course, wanted to cycle to school, too. But Uncle Roger said definitely not; it was too far. Nige was furious.

* * *

The first weekend mom had made up Kate's bed for Col. The curtains she threw out. They'd "had it," she reckoned—the moths had been at them. But it didn't matter because it was dark long before the boys would be going to

bed. Nick helped her put the little bed together, and tuck in the sheets and blankets.
They flung open the window to get rid of the
musty smell. The room seemed bright and
lived-in again. *And I'll be able to show Col my fox's
head, too!* Nick thought. . . . *We should be able to
patch it up all right, with a bit of glue.*

After that, Col came every weekend.

* * *

On the Saturday before Christmas the two
boys arrived at the farm to be told by Annie (up
to her elbows in flour because she was making
mince pies) that Tom was away at the church
practicing carols. Nick knew mom was down at
church, too, helping with the decorations. So
the boys decided they'd be able to sneak off for
a really long ride—by themselves—and, if they
were careful, no one would ever know.

Nick had a special reason for wanting to do
this. "Col, it's just that, well, Kate and I went off
with mom's new washing line that day, and it'd
be good to go up and . . . but someone's probably gone off with it by now. All the same, shall
we go and have a look?"

"What? Up by the lake on Castle How?"

The weather was gray but warm for De-
cember. No danger of storms or icy rocks.
Funnily enough, Krow had become much
more friendly since Nick had started riding
him. They caught him with no trouble at all.

There were no other houses on the Fawcetts' side of the valley so the boys had no trouble in sneaking down through the meadows—with a rather sleepy Krow—to the creek at the bottom. They'd decided to cross it at a wide, shallow place. But Krow wasn't keen at all, and although Nick'd planned to ride across (while Col got wet leading him!), in the end they both had to wade and pull, shove, and heave to get the little colt's hairy legs into the icy, swift-flowing water.

After they'd crossed, they set off briskly to warm themselves. They kept to the edge of a little wood that ran up the side of the valley; it gave them shelter. They wouldn't be seen that way.

Nick was determined to make the most of this last weekend of being the only one to ride Krow. He even meant to ride him right up the fellside. But as it got steeper he found himself slithering down the pony's glossy back. He only stayed on board at all by grabbing a fistful of scrubby mane. Then Krow went on strike. Stopped dead. Refused to move. After all, he loved fellsides, but he wasn't so stupid that he was going to cart a boy up this one!

So Nick let go and slid off into the crisp, brown bracken. Then all three of them—on all fours most of the time—staggered off up the massive slope.

This time the patchwork of fields that unfolded below them wasn't greens but browns and fawns, and the woods showed up like meshes of gray. They climbed by tiny, winding sheep paths. Krow seemed to know the way. Soon the hot, sticky smell of his sweaty coat mixed with the smell of peat and bogwater.

As they struggled over the top of the hill they saw the lake. Krow plowed on, pulling Nick who was holding the rope from his halter. The pony didn't stop till he'd reached the edge of the lake. It was partly iced-over now; the surface had melted and frozen again to form a crazy zigzag pattern. The reeds had sunk into the warmer mud on the bottom. Not a creature was to be seen.

Krow was thirsty after his climb. He stopped on the crisp mud and stretched his neck out towards the ice.

Then—perhaps he remembered games he'd played the previous winter—he raised one front hoof high in the air, crashed it into the ice, and leapt back sharply at the clatter he'd made.

He knocked Nick flying. Col staggered but held onto the rope as Nick dropped it. The echo of the crash was sounding, sounding, around the surrounding crags. Then Nick remembered.

"KROW!" he yelled. "KROW!"

"Krow, Krow, Krow . . ." the crags answered back. The pony looked at Nick in astonishment. He looked very funny now; he'd gotten bracken shoots in his mane, poking up between his ears.

Then, as they sat there with the pony standing near them, Nick told Colin the last secret of all. The one about Krow-with-a-*K*. "I'd hardly know how to spell the wretched word anyway!" Colin laughed.

Still sweaty from the climb, they lay back on the pale grass, watching the rapid gusts of steamy air churning from Krow's nostrils.

I must remember, Nick was thinking, *to tell Uncle Roger he was right about me going onto the high fells again before the year was out. I've done it—with eleven days to spare!*

Then they wandered slowly backwards and forwards with Krow across the empty spaces, looking for the missing rope. Yes, it *was* there, just where they'd left it four months before. Being nylon, it was none the worse for the rain, but the paper Co-op tags looked like drops of porridge.

Nick hooked the rope carefully over Krow's neck, but as soon as they began to move down the steep slope again, the coils snaked over the pony's lowered head and writhed into a heap in front of his hooves. Again they had to laugh at the look on his face.

"Hey—holly!" Nick had caught sight of a clump of knotty little trees behind one of the walls. The dark mass was covered with tiny, scarlet dots.

"Look, why not . . . with a rope and a 'pack horse'? And I've got a knife me dad sometimes takes with him in the truck." Colin scrambled over the wall before he'd finished speaking.

Nick stayed with Krow on the other side. The knife was sharp. Soon Col was tossing branches over to them and a spikey, bouncy pile grew on the grass. Krow tried a nibble but curled his lips back in disgust at the sharpness of the prickles.

When Col clambered back, they set about fastening one end of the rope around the largest branch. The idea was to pass the other end around Krow's belly, then the rest of the bundle, finally tying it onto the end of the main branch again. Squealing with agony, Colin clutched the prickly bundle and held it above Krow's back while Nick let go of the halter rope and scrambled around trying to get the right bits of washing line in the right places.

Talk about a pair of idiots! As soon as the prickles settled onto Krow he felt them, too! And he didn't even bother to squeal. He just plunged away, and in seconds the top of his flying tail was disappearing around a corner of the wall. The boys stared after him for a moment. Then they collapsed with laughing.

It seemed such a shame to leave all those fabulous pieces of holly when the Braithwaites' house was just there, below them. They still had the rope, so they made a sling with it and carried the prickly bundle between them.

Krow was waiting for them by the side gate. Mom was holding him as he grazed peacefully on the sweet, green grass. "What on earth are you two guys up to?" she laughed as the boys stumbled into sight, singing "The Holly and the Ivy" at the tops of their voices. "I just saw this black thing rocketing down the slope while I was walking back from church up the path here," she went on, "and something told me it must be your Krow. But where on earth will we put all that beautiful holly? . . . Well, put it in the shed for now, and come and have your tea!"

"OK, mom!" They hauled their load around to the back of the house, while mom fastened Krow's halter rope to a bush so that he could crop the rough grass by the front drive.

Then—at last—tea and the first plate of mince pies that she'd made.

"Trouble is," she told them as they stuffed their mouths full of sweet, crumbly pastry, "no one down at the church could find the crib we use for the manger scene. It just isn't anywhere. So I was thinking, you two. If only you could get Krow's finished, ready for the play at church on Tuesday. I mean, what if Colin stayed for a few days to help? What *are* you doing over Christmas anyway, Col?"

Colin knew—and Nick knew—that Mrs. Stokes was going to be working in the hotel, and his dad would be fetching a load from London with his truck. But Nick hadn't dared ask mom, what with the money problem and everyone else they'd asked over on Christmas Day—Uncle Rog, Aunt Meg, Nigel.

But this way they didn't have to ask. Within minutes mom had decided. Col must spend Christmas with them. That way, both boys could get the manger finished by Tuesday, and they could pin up all that holly together.

It struck Nick that it was a rather good idea that his manger should hold the Christ baby in the stable scene, before being given to Tom as a present on Christmas Day. After all, it was partly because of Tom that he had had a "new" life, a fresh start. Yes, Nick liked the idea very much.

"But look, you two," mom finally said. "If you don't take Tom's precious fell pony back to him soon, he'll be wondering if he's ever going to see him again—let alone wanting a manger for him to eat out of! And," she added with a smile as the boys stampeded to the door with the trimmings of the mince-pie pastry for Krow, "I wouldn't mind having that washing line back, either, when you've finished with it!"

So she had recognized it all the time! Nick smiled back. "OK, mom!"

As the door slammed, she began piling up the empty plates. When the boys returned from the farm, she decided, she'd tell them about that letter she'd had that morning: from dad, saying he'd be back just in time for Christmas, and was longing to see them all.